# HITCHED

## STEELE RANCH - BOOK 4

## VANESSA VALE

Hitched

ISBN: 978-1-7959-0007-2

Cover design: Bridger Media

Cover graphic: Bigstock: marconicouto, fotorince; Deposit Photo: cokacoka

# GET A FREE BOOK!

JOIN MY MAILING LIST TO BE THE FIRST TO KNOW OF NEW
RELEASES, FREE BOOKS, SPECIAL PRICES AND OTHER
AUTHOR GIVEAWAYS.

http://freeromanceread.com

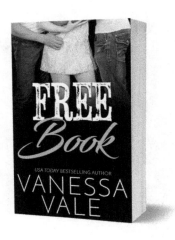

# ILDER

JANUARY IN MONTANA was cold as fuck. After a day of riding snowmobiles in the bright sunshine but close to zero temperatures, it felt good to be settled in front of a roaring fire, whiskey in hand. It paid to be friends with Micah and Colt, wilderness outfitters who had taken us on an awesome day into the national forest. There was nothing like seeing the great outdoors seated on two-hundred horsepower, but when we returned to Hawk's Landing where we were staying for the weekend, we'd discovered the indoors was just as wild.

A man in leather pants and a snug black t-shirt led a woman by a leash. She wore a red leather skirt the size of a Band-Aid and a black bustier that made her breasts defy gravity. Yup, a leash. She had a collar about her neck and was content to follow a few steps behind, eyes down as they made their way to the resort's conference room that had been converted for the night into a BDSM dungeon. A group from Billings had rented out the resort for the weekend—except for our two rooms. A dominatrix wearing black boots with lethal stiletto heels and a latex top had a man crawling behind her in the same direction across the resort's great room. Thankfully, the two-story stone fireplace was lit and the heat had been set a touch warmer than usual since he wore nothing but a metal cock cage over his dick. The sight had me wincing and shifting on the leather couch. I didn't mind a woman playing with my dick or my balls, but I liked a gentler approach—and the ability to come.

Unfortunately, the only woman I wanted anywhere near my dick wouldn't be caught dead in fet wear. No, she was too sweet, too pure. Too innocent for anything as wild and kinky as what was happening tonight. Sarah Gandry was the woman I wanted to marry, not the woman I fucked in a dungeon. Well, I *wanted* to fuck her pretty much anywhere, but it turned out we weren't compatible. At least, that was what she thought. I found her smart as fuck, gorgeous and perfect. Oh, and I loved her.

Shit, I shifted my dick in my jeans just thinking about her. She had gorgeous black hair and the perfect, very fuckable body. I'd never forget her plump lips. Yeah, she might not have my cock in a restraint, but she'd been leading me around by it for years.

And not just me, she had King pussy-whipped, too. And we hadn't gotten anywhere near that pussy of hers.

"When I heard about the event this weekend, I was going to cancel, but we figured you'd be fine with this going on," Micah said, leaning back in the big leather couch, feet on the coffee table, his glass of whiskey resting on his chest. He angled his head toward the fet event that was happening in a room behind him, the thumping of a deep base from Nine Inch Nails muted. "While you don't live the lifestyle anymore, you aren't bothered by it. Wouldn't say shit about what you see."

King shrugged from the chair beside mine, lifted his glass in salute. The furniture was set up in a U-shape in front of the fireplace, Micah facing it directly, us perpendicular.

King grinned. "Bothered? Hell, no. We just wish our girl was into it like we are, although neither of us have been to an event like this in a long time. As for letting anyone watch? I don't care what others do, whatever floats their boat and all that. But if—"

"When," I said, cutting him off.

"—when" —he corrected himself— "we get our girl between us, we're not sharing her with others. No part of her. Not her gorgeous body, the sounds she makes or how she looks when she comes."

"No fucking way," I added, getting pissed just thinking of some bastard seeing Sarah like that. "That shit belongs to us."

Yeah, *our* girl. King and I had been best friends since kindergarten and we'd wanted Sarah for years, since before she was even legal. Watched out for her longer than that. Being six years older, we'd bided our time—we might be into kink, but we didn't go for jail bait—until she'd finished college and returned to Barlow, to date her. Separately, so we didn't scare her off. Dinner, movies, bowling. Chaste kisses at her front door.

God, they'd been sweet, but it had been almost impossible not to push her up against her front door, nudge my thigh between hers and feel the heat of her pussy even through my jeans as I took her mouth in a claiming kiss. That's what I'd wanted to do with her. Sink into her and lose my mind, make her lose hers.

But she hadn't been interested. She hadn't responded to the brush of my lips against her brow, along the corner of her mouth. No gasp of breath, no clench of fingers on my biceps. No lifting her face to mine for more.

No, she hadn't been interested in the tender attentions either of us showed her and had ultimately turned us down, one after the other. Strange, because we'd been sure she'd been into us. Every time we ran into her, interest had flared in her eyes, her cheeks had turned pink. And when I'd picked her up at the door, she'd been eager. But by the end of the date, nothing. Just a small smile, a quick thank you before she'd gone inside and closed the door in my face. King had said the same had happened to him.

The rejection had stung, and still did. It was confusing because up until I'd walked her to the door we'd had a good time. Being with Sarah felt like being home. It was always easy, no nervous silences. We'd known each other so well already. And yet...no desire. No passion, as I'd hoped. As King had hoped, too. But that didn't mean we didn't stop wanting her. No, we were men who got what we wanted, and we wanted Sarah. We just had to be patient and think of our next plan of attack.

Micah grinned. "I didn't know you had a girl. Congrats."

King's smile slipped. "We don't," he grumbled. "Well, we *do*, but she doesn't know it yet." He took a sip of his drink. "We want a relationship like yours."

"What?" Micah frowned, suddenly wary. "With a movie star?"

"Fuck, Micah, you know us better than that," I told him. Obviously, he was protective of his wife. "We don't give a shit that Lacey's famous. We want a woman to share like you and Colt do. Like Matt and Ethan, too," I added, referring to the resort's owners. The two men shared a wife as well. Rachel.

"Not just any woman, we want to share Sarah," King clarified, lifting a finger from the side of his glass and pointed. "We just have to figure out how to get her."

Damned straight. There was interest there, even if she'd said no to additional dates. Her eyes lit up when she saw me—and I stopped by the library for more than books—but that hadn't swayed her into another date. It made no sense.

"Tell me about her," Micah said, taking a sip of his drink. His gold wedding ring glinted in the firelight and I was envious as fuck of that simple outward gesture of his commitment to Lacey.

I ran a hand over my face, realized I probably should have shaved because my five o'clock shadow was heading toward a beard. We'd returned from snowmobiling, showered in our rooms, ate a big meal in the dining room and were now relaxing by the fire. The only thing better than this would be if Sarah were with us. Between us. *Under* us.

"She grew up in Barlow with a crazy-ass mother and younger half-brother. How she turned out normal I have no idea," I told him, wondering if her mother was on her third or fourth husband by now. Maybe even fifth. She changed husbands as fast as most people changed the oil in their car. Instead of working, she married rich men, divorced them for a big settlement and moved on.

"Sarah went off to college in Bozeman, came back and got the job as the town librarian when the lady who'd been there since forever retired," King added. He leaned forward, grabbed the whiskey bottle we'd pulled from the hotel bar and refilled his glass with about two fingers of the amber liquid. He'd changed out of his heavy winter-wear for a blue flannel shirt, jeans and leather boots. His pale hair was slicked back from his shower, but had curled at the ends from the heat from the fireplace.

"Smart and the most amazing smile you've ever seen." If Micah wanted to know about Sarah, we'd tell him. "She's tiny, doesn't even come up to my shoulder." I put my hand up as if to measure her. "Sleek black hair that goes halfway down her back. Curves in all the right places." My hand shifted as I used it to form the shape of an hourglass.

"Don't forget the damned dimple," King added. Micah's gaze turned his way as King pointed to his right cheek. "That fucking dimple can bring a man to his knees."

"But she's not interested," Micah repeated.

King sighed and I took a big swallow of my drink, let it burn its way down to my stomach.

"Nope," King said. "We took her out, separately. We didn't want to scare her with our intentions of claiming her together even though we've known her forever. Except for you guys around here in Bridgewater, it's not like having two men interested in you is the norm. A few men we know in Barlow share a woman as well, but it's not like Sarah would know about it. Expect it. She was interested. I know it. I felt it, saw it in her eyes, yet she turned me down for a third date."

"Me, too," I added. I had to wonder if she'd been scared, if we'd somehow pushed her too hard. Perhaps because her mother was so...bold with her affections with men, it had made Sarah inhibited. I was willing to go as slow as she needed, as long as she *did* need. Us.

I sighed. It was fucking frustrating because I loved her. Wanted her. *Needed* her. We'd waited long enough and now...now she was driving me crazy.

Micah put his glass on a coaster on the end table. "If she's not into you, then why not see if there are any single subs at the party? Nothing wrong with scratching that itch with a willing woman if you're single. Especially that need to dominate." His gaze lifted and he looked over King's head toward the reception area. "You guys like petite and curvy? Dark haired? There's a woman talking with Rachel who fits your type."

I huff out a laugh. "While my dick is tired of my hand," I admitted, "it doesn't have any interest in anyone besides—"

"What the fuck?" King said quietly. He'd shifted in his seat and was looking toward the reception desk.

I spun about at his tone and the way his eyes were practically popping out of his head. My brain couldn't process what I was seeing, yet the words fell from my mouth.

"No. Fucking. Way."

Sarah. In the flesh. And a whole lot of it. A black latex skirt caught the light and made it shimmer. The cut was wide, like...like a fifties skirt without the puffy petticoat beneath. Hell, I didn't know shit about skirts. This one fell to a few inches above her knees. It wasn't indecent, but I'd never seen so much of Sarah's legs before. Ever. The black shoes she wore had a little strap across the front, almost school girl style, although the high heels made them anything but. They only showed off the toned legs even better. And that was just her lower half. She had on a prim white blouse, but it was short enough to show off a narrow strip of her pale waist and tied in the front. I only saw her in profile as she spoke with a woman behind the reception desk, Rachel, I assumed, but I could tell that a number of buttons were undone. Too many. Her sleek hair was back in a simple braid, as if she intended for someone to grab hold of it as they flipped up her skirt and fucked her from behind.

I shot up from the couch, stalked around it. I heard footsteps behind me and knew King followed.

"Sarah," I said. The one word shot from my mouth like a bullet and it made her turn on her high heels.

Her gorgeous eyes widened, her mouth fell open, her

pale skin went almost white, then she flushed as red as the lipstick on her full lips.

Facing me, I saw even more of her outfit. While the skirt covered her, her top did not. It was as if she'd taken one of her prim librarian blouses, skipped doing the buttons and tied it at the bottom to hold it closed. Beneath, a black lace bustier could be seen through the gaping part in the white fabric. But that wasn't all. Because the blouse was thin, it was blatantly obvious that the bra was a half cup style that didn't cover her nipples because I could see their dark color and how hard they were through it. And if I could see, then—

My jaw clenched and my dick swelled in my pants.

"Wilder," she breathed. She looked left, then right, as if she were considering ways to escape.

I felt more than saw King come to stand beside me.

"King," she added, her pink tongue darting out to lick her lips.

I crossed my arms over my chest.

"What are you doing here?" she asked, her voice a mix of breathy seductress and the squeak of Minnie Mouse. Her hands went to her skirt, smoothed it down, although it didn't need it, then went to her top, tucked the two halves together.

"Are we the only ones you don't want to see your nipples?" I asked, angling with my chin to indicate her sudden modesty. It pissed me off because all that gorgeous skin, those lush curves, were meant for me and King. And she was flaunting it for others to see.

Her eyes narrowed and she tapped her toe on the tile floor. "I'm here for the BDSM night."

It was King's turn to look around. I saw the way his jaw ticked. "Are you here with someone? Your dom?"

She didn't have a collar around her neck, the blatant sign she'd been claimed. The idea that she'd had a man on the side...a fucking dominant, made me see red. While we'd only dated, and casually at that, I—both of us—expected complete and total monogamy. But we weren't dating now. That had been months ago.

I was glad King asked the question because all I wanted to do was toss her over my shoulder, take her to my room and for us to show her how two men could top her. But she didn't want that. Or did she?

I wanted her, and for more than a quick fuck. I wanted all of her. Her smiles, her tears. Her joys and sorrows. The whole fucking deal. But she'd hidden herself from us, it seemed. She'd hidden a whole fucking lot, and I didn't mean those big tits that would more than fill my palms. We'd stayed away because we'd thought she was one thing, a shy virgin too timid to handle our darker needs, but now? No fucking way.

It seemed she had darker needs. Big secrets.

I loved her and I'd discover the true Sarah, kink and all. And if she already had a man, someone to give her what she needed, then...fine. No, it wasn't fucking fine. But I'd know the truth at least. We weren't her lovers, but I liked to think we were her friends. We deserved honesty, at least.

"No...I'm friends with Rachel." Sarah thumbed over her shoulder at the woman who was watching us closely. Rachel gave a small smile and a finger wave. "She told me about the event and I decided to um...check it out."

No man. No dom. Thank fuck. I inwardly sighed, but we weren't done. She wanted to *check out* a BDSM night? That meant— "Princess, you want men to dominate you, all you had to do was ask. You didn't have to drive all the way to Bridgewater."

Her mouth opened and closed a few times as if she didn't know what to say. We'd been calling her princess for years, but now, it meant something different, something more. Rachel, behind her, laughed. While my gaze didn't stray from Sarah, I saw Micah move to lean against the registration desk. I wasn't sure if he was there to watch out for Sarah—even though he knew we would never lay a hand on her in anger—or keep Rachel from leaping over it and protecting her friend, although she didn't seem too worried. Either way, I was glad he was there. It was time to get to the bottom of...everything, and Micah knew us, knew the rules of BDSM play.

Sarah's dark eyes flicked from mine to King and back. "Men. You mean—what?"

I smiled, stepped closer. Her grip got tighter on her blouse and she had to tilt her head back to look at me.

"Men. Me and King. While we've known you for a long time, it seems like there's some things we need to clear up."

Like the fact that our woman wanted it wild. She didn't want mild, like we'd been with her. That was fucking obvious now. She was fucking wearing an open-cupped bra.

"But—"

I cut her off. She'd led us about until now. It was time to change that.

"Are you afraid of us?"

She frowned. "You and King? I've known you forever. Of course not."

"Do you trust us?" King added.

Her dark gaze shifted to his.

"Yes." Her answer was immediate, no waffling or second guessing.

"Micah, did you hear that?" I asked, watching Sarah.

"I did," he replied.

"Good." Micah had heard Sarah's confidence in us, that she would be safe with us. While we wouldn't hurt a hair on her head, we'd stepped into BDSM without expecting it and needed to follow some protocol. Micah knew Sarah was with us, that she'd verbally shared with him and Rachel that she trusted us, that she wasn't afraid to be with us.

Done.

So I did what I'd wanted to do for...forever, leaned down and tossed her over my shoulder. I turned, headed toward the central stairway leading to the guest rooms on the second floor. Her hands pounded on my lower back as I cupped her thighs to keep her in place. "Wilder!"

I stopped halfway across the large room. "What's your safe word, princess?"

She stilled and went silent. I waited. Waited some more. I wasn't doing anything until she knew she was consenting to this, that we would give her exactly what she wanted, what she needed and nothing more.

"Red."

Relief coursed through me at that one word. Continuing toward my room, King on our heels, I knew that nothing was going to be the same again. I had Sarah in my arms and I was never letting her go. She could say red and everything would stop, but for once, we'd talk shit out. And until she said that one safe word, she belonged to us. She would do what we said or get her ass spanked. We'd make her ours, however kinky she wanted it.

## 2

ARAH

RED. *Red.* I'd never had a safe word before. Never imagined being asked that question. Never imagined being asked that question by *Wilder.* Sweet, thoughtful, intense, broody Wilder. But he had.

I was dressed like I was headed into a party with a bunch of BDSM experts. Which I had been until Wilder tossed me over his shoulder and headed the opposite direction.

While I might look ready to drop to my knees for a dominant in the party, looks were deceiving. I *was* into kink. I *was* interested in BDSM. I *was* interested in learning more about it, whether there was anything that might happen in the party that made me hot, that made me want a guy to do whatever I saw to me. I might not have had sex before, but I knew what I wanted.

I wanted it wild. Rough. I wanted to be pinned down, tied up, bent over, on my knees. I wanted all of that not because I read a bunch of romance novels or watched porn.

No, I wanted it because...I *wanted* it. I'd known pretty much forever that I was a little different. I never played wedding with my Barbie dolls. I would bind her hands together behind her back with a rubber band. I didn't put fancy outfits on her. I kept her naked. I'd thought darker thoughts even before I really knew what sex was. I couldn't explain it, still couldn't, but I just knew I was wired slightly differently. There wasn't any other way I could think of to explain it. It wasn't as if I could chat with my girlfriends about it. *Why did I want to be pinned down and fucked?* Yeah, that wouldn't have gone over well at a slumber party.

Missionary wasn't enough, even for my first time. And that was why I hadn't ever *had* a first time. I hadn't found the right guy to know what I needed, or for me to be comfortable enough with him to *tell* him what I needed.

And that included Wilder and King. I'd been in love with both of them since I was thirteen, the summer before seventh grade. The first time I saw them was at my mother's third wedding reception. This was the marriage to a rich rancher, King's family's neighbor. Since my mother had married a local—that time—everyone from Barlow had been invited. Pretty much everyone had gone too, including Wilder and King.

The only reason I could think that two nineteen-year-olds would want to go to a wedding reception was easy access to alcohol. It had been when Danny Sayers had gotten me behind a tree and put his hand on my barely developed chest over my top, and I'd pushed him off that they'd appeared and scared the crap out of him. While they hadn't laid a finger on poor Danny, he'd gotten a lesson on how to treat a lady—even a thirteen-year-old one—and when no meant no. He'd been in my class all the way through graduation, but he hadn't spoken to me once after that day. Barely even looked at me.

All through school, I'd never thought about him, or any boy. All I saw, with teenage stars in my eyes, were Wilder and King. Yes, both of them. Perhaps that was the first sign that I knew I was different. I'd crushed after two men. And they had been *men*. Tall, muscled, intensely focused. One dark, the other fair. One lean, the other broad. Gorgeous. For years I would touch myself, make myself come to fantasies of them taking me, touching me. Hell, fucking me.

When it came to my orgasms, no one else would do, it seemed.

My youthful crush shifted to adult love. By the time I'd returned home from college and settled in at my job at the town library, I saw them frequently. Wilder was a particularly avid reader and checked books out several times a week.

The town was small and it was hard to miss them, or anyone else. Besides the library, I saw King often at the grocery store, one time at the gas station and even at the dentist—Wilder's dad used to be my dentist, but a woman had bought his practice when he'd retired.

I may have been off-limits for a long time, but the age difference wasn't so important any longer. I was twenty-three. A woman and well past legal. Fortunately, they didn't look at me as if I were a child any longer. Their gazes were always dark, heated. Interested. I had no doubt of that.

I'd dated, but no one had been of interest and they'd never become a *boyfriend*. Then, I'd dated them.

First, Wilder had asked me out, and I'd been so excited. Nervous and thrilled, hoping he'd do everything I'd imagined. But he'd been...tame. Gentlemanly, but mild. I hadn't seen the look of a man who wanted to devour a woman. We'd had fun, one time we'd gone bowling and another time on a picnic by the river. I liked his conversation, his personality. He'd made me laugh. I'd liked...no, loved everything about him, except there had been no chemistry.

It was the exact same thing with King when he'd asked me out the following month. We'd gone on a few dates. He'd shown me kindness. He'd been...sweet. Blah.

Their kisses had been chaste. No tongue, no feeling. No ravishing. While it hadn't been brotherly, it hadn't been hot either. I hadn't gotten wet. My nipples hadn't gotten hard. There hadn't been any kind of zing.

While my heart and pussy might pine for them, my head told me no. I wasn't going to be stuck with a man who didn't excite me sexually, who wouldn't give me what I needed, even though I didn't know exactly what that was.

Because of this, I'd turned them down for future dates. That had been hard. Very hard, the winter so far long and boring. There'd been crying involved, lots of donuts and wine. Lots of heartache every time I saw them in town, every time Wilder came to the library. But Rachel—my friend from college—had invited me to come to the BDSM weekend at the resort she ran with her husbands to try the party and have fun. She'd said I didn't have to do anything, that no one would touch me without my permission. That had comforted me and I'd needed to look beyond Barlow to possibly find a man who could get me wet, get me wild. Bridgewater wasn't too far and if I were ever going to find someone, I had to get out there. Staying in my PJs with a book and hot cocoa wasn't going to do it.

While Rachel and her husbands weren't into BDSM, or at least not in a group setting, she *did* have *two* husbands. Two. So for the party tonight, she was to be my wingman and Matt and Ethan would be hers—as if those huge, doting men would leave her side. We'd only be observing, although I had no doubt by the end of the night, with their baby asleep, they'd be in their bedroom having their own private party of three.

Still, Rachel had told me I couldn't show up in my usual attire of jeans and blouses and had offered to order clothes for me online, just for the party. *Clothes* wasn't the right word for what she'd had delivered. Scraps of fabric, that's what my seventy dollars had paid for. While the flared skirt made of latex swirled down to mid-thigh, it had been the bustier she'd gotten me that I'd freaked about. The bra was only half-cups and it must have been at a bargain price since half the material was missing. My nipples weren't even covered! When I'd put it on and gotten a good look at myself, I'd questioned our friendship. Why would Rachel think I'd be okay with something so revealing in front of a roomful of strangers? And her husbands? God, I'd almost died thinking of Matt and Ethan seeing me like that. I'd never be able to look them in the eye again.

That was why I'd put my own white blouse back on and covered up, even though I looked like a petite, curvy Britney Spears. I might want to watch the party from the sidelines, but I had no plans to do so with my nipples on display.

To make matters worse, Rachel didn't have a special outfit. No, she wore jeans and a Hawk's Landing shirt, telling me her men wouldn't let her expose her body to anyone but them. I seriously questioned our friendship.

I'd expected to see some interesting things at the party. I'd prepared myself not to show surprise or horror or too much curiosity, depending on what the couples did. It wasn't my place to judge or question what consenting adults chose to do, especially since they were in solid relationships, trusting each other enough to participate in a BDSM event. I didn't even have a relationship.

So when I saw the guy with his dick in a cage crawling toward the party following behind his mistress, I wasn't *too* surprised. But I hadn't expected to see Wilder and King. *They* were a total shock. I swore my heart skipped a beat when I heard Wilder's voice call out my name in a deep, dark tone.

I'd practically hyperventilated watching as they crossed the great room, eyes focused squarely and solely on me. My heart began beating double-time, my palms became damp, my nipples hardened and my pussy got wet between one quick breath and the next.

They'd been surprised to see me, yes. Stunned, even. I'd expected revulsion, shame, even embarrassment on their expressions as they studied me in my slutty outfit, but no.

No. The banked heat I used to see in their eyes when they looked at me had returned. Only hotter. Brighter. More obvious.

They wanted me. It was blatant, even to me.

And now I was tossed over Wilder's shoulder and all I could see was his gorgeous ass, his worn jeans molding it perfectly.

"Wilder," I said again.

I saw King's lower legs, his boots, as he walked behind us. Wilder stopped, moved to the side and it was when a couple's legs came and went from my upside-down view that I knew we hadn't been alone in the upstairs hallway. Since the resort was filled solely with guests participating in the BDSM activities this weekend, they probably hadn't thought anything of a woman tossed over a man's shoulder. *This* was tame.

Wilder started walking again. "Here's what's going to happen, princess," he began.

God, I'd always loved it when they'd called me that.

"We're going to my room and you're going to tell us what the hell is going on. You have your safe word. Use it. Otherwise you do what we say. Understand?"

I was quiet as I processed his words, bumping along over his shoulder.

"Princess, answer me." A light swat fell on my upper thigh. Nothing painful, but it tingled. And was really hot.

"Yes, I understand," I replied, speaking the words to his lower back.

He paused and I heard a door opening. He went into a room, the light came on, King closing the door behind us. I heard the snick of the deadbolt as I was lowered back to my feet. My hands went immediately to my skirt, smoothing it back down over my thighs. Wilder's big hand remained on my waist as I adjusted to being upright again. I could feel the callouses against the bare strip of my belly.

While I had often fantasized what it would be like being alone in a hotel room with Wilder and King, I'd never thought it would actually happen.

There was a king-sized bed, a small table and chair, and a low dresser with a flat-screen TV on top. The motif was western with lots of wood, including the log headboard. The carpet and curtains were a dark navy, a large-print western landscape was on the wall by the bathroom. It was just like mine, although I had a smaller bed.

King moved to stand beside Wilder, shoulder to shoulder once again. But in this space, instead of the two-story great room, I felt small. Tiny, in fact. I took a step back and King sighed at my retreat. He moved to the bed, sat on the edge. Wilder followed, sat a few feet away. I had to turn around to continue to face them, but they were my height now and not as imposing.

"You're into BDSM?" King asked, his gaze raking over every inch of me, then settling on mine. Held.

I licked my lips. "Maybe."

"Good girl, I like the truth."

"Why would I lie?" I asked King, tilting my head to the side.

"Why would you hide the truth from us?" he returned.

My eyes narrowed, studying them. King was fair, his hair the color of wheat. In the summer, it lightened from the sun. His whiskers were a touch darker, and while he wasn't close-shaven, I wouldn't call the scruff on his square jaw a beard either. It only made him look rugged. It was his eyes, so pale as to be almost the color of ice, which had caught me all those years ago. And still did.

As for Wilder, he was the romance novel's tall, dark and handsome hero. His hair was longer, unruly but not messy. His eyes were dark, his gaze intense. He was the serious one while King was more lighthearted, but the way the two of them eyed me now, they were equally focused.

They were big. So big. Wide shoulders, but King was broader like the football player he'd once been. Wilder was leaner, but no less muscled. He reminded me of a runner with his trim physique. Both were well over a head taller than me; I only came up to their chins, and that had been while wearing these ridiculously high heels. I wanted to run my hands over both of them, feel those muscles shift and bunch, hear the beating of their hearts, their deep breaths. I wanted to get close enough to breathe in their scents; King liked a soap that smelled like the woods while Wilder didn't use any kind of scent. I wanted to put my nose at the crook of his neck and breathe him in.

And their lips...I'd felt them. Soft, warm, but gentle. Too damned gentle. I wanted all their power. No restraint.

I just wanted...them. I loved them, always had and now that they were sitting before me, knew I always would.

"The truth?" I asked. "I wasn't hiding it from you specifically, but it's private, something I only want to share with my—" I stumbled then, looking away. Embarrassed.

"Who, princess? Your lover?" Wilder asked.

I nodded, thankful he said the word for me. But I didn't have a lover. While the room wasn't cold, it was chillier than the great room with the wonderful fireplace. Goosebumps rose on my arms.

"What do you like? Bondage? Whips? Spanking? Floggers?" he questioned.

King added to the list. "Anal? Nipple clamps? Deep submission like master/slave?"

My eyes whipped to his at the last. *Slave?*

"No!" I replied quickly. I didn't want to be anyone's slave, under anyone's thumb. I'd had enough of that with my mother. I just ached for someone to...make me forget. To clear my thoughts like cobwebs from my mind and fill my head with nothing but him. *Them.*

"No?" King asked, his eyes lowering to my chest again. His gaze heated, the blue darkening. "Your outfit definitely says *something.*"

I tilted my chin up in defiance. "My outfit doesn't say slave. Besides, I can wear whatever I want." Not that I'd be caught dead in this outfit again. God, it was humiliating enough with these two seeing me like this. Coming to Hawk's Landing was supposed to be anonymous. So much for that.

"That's right, you can. Your outfit doesn't say slave, because a slave would be naked."

My eyes widened at that clarification.

"But if you're offering what that outfit shows, then you didn't have to come all the way to Bridgewater, princess," King told her, pointing at my clothing. "As Wilder said, all you had to do was ask and we'd take care of you."

I tugged my shirt closed, then realized I could do up the buttons now. Rachel wasn't going to scoff at me for being a prude at a BDSM event. She wasn't one to talk in her unisex golf shirt and pants though. We so weren't friends anymore.

Fumbling with the buttons, I got them done so that I was covered in white cotton from neck to knotted hem. I tugged at that, pulled the tails loose and let the blouse drop so that it fell over the waistband of my skirt, and now at least my midriff was covered.

The men were quiet and watched me do this. Only when I dropped my hands to my sides did they say more. "We can still see your nipples, princess. That thin fabric is practically transparent and the bra does nothing to hide them," Wilder said.

I crossed my arms over my chest, felt the hard points that they'd seen. I usually wore my nude colored bra, the one that had padding. But a black half-cup? God, where was the hole to drop into?

"You're beautiful, princess," King added. "We like

seeing you dressed like this. It's sexy as hell. We just don't like seeing you dressed like this in front of others."

"Possessive much?" I asked, tapping my toe again.

King grinned. "Fuck, yes. Those berry-tipped breasts are just for us. That pale skin by your navel? Just for us to lick and kiss." His eyes dropped lower, his smile slipped. "And those hips—"

"Perfect to grip as I fuck you from behind," Wilder added.

"Or grip as she sits on my face," King added.

"But..." I sputtered, confused and almost startled by their words. Or at least those words from *them*.

My cheeks flared hot for a different reason. They were talking dirty. Really dirty. About me. About doing things to me. I'd dreamed of them speaking this way to me, but they never had. Until now.

"Do you like those things, princess? Of us doing them to you?" Wilder asked, his voice louder, pushier.

I was flustered, confused, overwhelmed. I was thinking about Wilder gripping my hips as he fucked me from behind, but when King added that about his mouth on me as I...God, I couldn't think. I blurted out, "I don't know!"

"That's right," Wilder said, his voice quiet. "You don't know, do you, princess, because you've been a good girl and never let a man have what belongs to us. That pussy is tight and untried, your cherry just waiting for us to take."

## 3

# S ARAH

"Yes!" I said, covering my face with my hands, too afraid to look at them now that I'd admitted the truth. How sad was it that I'd waited all this time for them, for something I didn't even know they wanted as much as me? I took a deep breath. "I can't...I can't do this." I turned on my heel to leave, to hide. To run.

King stepped around me, blocked the door. "Say your safe word, princess, and we'll let you go. Otherwise, you do as we say."

"We haven't done anything to need a safe word," I countered. My hands trembled and my heart was beating frantically. I wasn't big on exercise, but I felt like I'd run a mile.

King's hand came up, his knuckles stroking gently

down my cheek. He'd done a similar gesture when he'd taken me out on a date last summer, but this felt... different. That the simple caress was a precursor to more and not *all* like I'd thought then.

"Sometimes talking about hard things is enough," he told me. "You know we're pushing you, right?"

I looked at his blue flannel shirt, noticed how the color matched his eyes, although I doubted he'd worn it for such a reason. "Why?"

"Because you're at a BDSM party wearing the sexiest fucking outfit I've ever seen. Last summer, you didn't even like either of us kissing you goodnight. Who's the real Sarah Gandry?"

*Who was the real Sarah Gandry?* That was a good question.

"What's your safe word?"

"Red."

King took a step closer, his hands going to the buttons I'd just done up on my shirt. Slowly, but deftly, he undid the top one. Met my gaze. "You don't want mild."

I sighed, not sure if it was because that was exactly correct or if it was because his knuckles brushed over the skin between my collarbones as they moved down to the second button.

"Neither do you," I countered.

"No, we don't. You want someone to take charge, to not wait for you to tell him it's okay. You'll tell him red when it's not. We'll be those men."

My eyelids fell closed as he moved to the next button, relaxing because he was right. That was exactly what I wanted and it seemed he was giving it to me, one button at a time. While I didn't want someone to push himself on me, I wanted him to...to lead, to test my boundaries, my desires in a safe environment, knowing I could say no through my safe word at any time. I didn't want to tell a man what I wanted because I didn't know what *it* was.

"Yes," I breathed.

I felt Wilder behind me, his hands going to my shoulders and when King finished with the final button on my blouse, he slid the fabric down so it fell to the floor at our feet.

I still didn't open my eyes. Didn't dare. I knew, even in the soft lighting, that they could see my breasts, see the tiny gold hoops pierced through them. The black bustier didn't cover much and lifted everything. I could feel their gazes on me.

"Holy fuck, Sarah," King said, his voice deep and rough. "How long have you had the piercings?"

"Two years," I replied.

"Jesus, we've seen you around town and you had these gorgeous nipple rings in all that time?"

I nodded. What else could I say?

"Every time you wore those prim librarian clothes you had these beneath?" He exhaled, as if trying to calm himself.

"Any hard limits, princess?" Wilder growled, his lips brushing over my shoulder.

Tilting my head to the side, I gave him room. *More.*

"I...I don't know." I paused. Thought, even as he kissed me, his tongue licking my skin. "Um, I don't want to be peed on."

I felt Wilder's smile against my shoulder, heard King's

chuckle. "That's good. We'd be the ones calling red if you did."

"No breath play. And I don't think I'd like to be fisted."

I shivered at the possibility. I'd seen King's and Wilder's hands, lusted after them touching me, but that didn't mean...nope.

Fingers brushed over my exposed nipples and my eyes flew open. King ran his knuckles over the sensitive tips. "Such a good girl, telling us this. Why didn't you say something last summer?"

"What? That I'm a virgin, into being with two men and kinky stuff, but don't want to be fisted?" It was my turn to laugh. "Yeah, you'd have run off faster than a jackrabbit."

"You forgot the nipple rings," King said, his gaze lowering, then flicking back to mine, kissed my temple, then my cheek, then the corner of my mouth.

"Right, I could've...I could've mentioned those, too." Where I'd been cold a minute ago, I was warm now. Hot, even. With them on both sides of me, their lips brushing over me, I felt closed in, but not claustrophobic. I felt engulfed. I felt...aroused.

"You're telling us these things now and you're not running," Wilder added.

I tilted my head to the side, looked up at him over my shoulder. His dark eyes were right there, watching me. Studying. Paying very close attention as if every breath, every move I made was important.

"Are you telling me you want me, that you want to do...things with me?" I asked.

Hands went to my upper arms and I was gently spun

about. Wilder leaned down, met my eyes with his dark ones. "Fuck, yes."

"Then why did you act all gentlemanly and...nice on those dates? And why did you date me separately?"

"We are gentlemen, princess. Just not in the bedroom," King said, flicking the small nipples rings with his fingers making them lift, then fall. I felt it inside my nipples and all the way to my toes. "We've known you forever, know how sweet and kind, smart and loving you are. We didn't want to scare you away."

I pursed my lips. "Thank you for telling me the truth," I said, repeating his earlier words. "But shouldn't I decide what's scary? Aren't I the one who says red?"

King's smiled twisted.

"What we want to do with you, to you, if you knew..." Wilder began, then let it drop.

I turned to face him, look in his eyes. "If I'd known, I'd have gone on more dates with *both* of you."

Wilder grabbed me, pulled me into his arms for a fierce hug. His chin settled on top of my head, the soft feel of his shirt against the top half of my bare breasts and nipples felt strange, but good. Intimate. "Fuck, princess. I've finally got you in my arms. You think I'm letting you go? No fucking way. You're mine."

"Ours," King added.

Hope rose up like balloons in the movie *Up*. So much of it that I felt it could lift a whole house. "Really?" I asked, happiness coursing through my veins along with the low thrum of arousal. I'd wanted to hear them say that since I was thirteen. Dreamed about it, touched myself thinking about it. And now...I had no intention of going anywhere. God, I wanted them.

With Wilder's arm wrapped about me, he walked me back to the bed and this time, sat beside me, his weight dipping the mattress so I leaned into him. "We've been too nice, haven't we? You want wild? It's our job to give it to you. You want gentle and slow, to have your cherry taken in one slow, wet thrust? It's our job to give it to you."

"I don't want that," I said, making sure he knew.

"You don't want us to pop that sweet cherry?"

The idea, the thought of Wilder's cock filling me, stretching me, ripping me wide open had me get even wetter. My panties had been totally ruined before, but now? Drenched.

"I do. I *so* do. I've...I've been saving it for you, like you said. Hoping it would be you."

"Wilder, or both of us?" King asked, settling on the other side of me so I was between them, just where I wanted to be.

I blushed hotly, but now that things had been said, there didn't seem to be any room for secrets any longer. "Both of you."

Perhaps they were mind readers, for Wilder said, "No more secrets, princess. If you want us to fuck you, to take you down a dark and dirty path of kinky pleasure, then you have to tell us everything."

"Okay," I replied.

"Okay?" King added. "What do you say to the men in charge in the bedroom?"

My mouth fell open and I shivered at the dark quality of his voice, the intensity in his eyes when I looked to him. King's gaze was heated, but it held more dominance and sharp focus than desire.

"Yes, sir."

"Good girl."

"That's right," Wilder added. "Such a good princess for your men."

I preened under their praise, the warmth of their words. I felt it in places that had been empty. In a matter of minutes, they'd been filled with the attentions and affection of not just one man, but two.

Wilder and King.

"Time to discover what gets you hot," Wilder said.

"And what gets you off," King added. His hand slid up my back, worked the clasp of my bra and unhooked it. It dropped to the crook of my elbows and my lap. I wasn't small, a solid D with large nipples. When Wilder groaned and King cursed under his breath as they stared at them fully exposed for the first time, I felt powerful in my own feminine way. I knew whatever they were going to do to me tonight I had some sway over them as well.

Each put a hand on a bare shoulder and pushed me back so I was on my back between them, my knees bent and my feet—still in my stilettos—on the carpeted floor.

"One more time, princess. What's your safe word?" King asked, looming over me. They both were. One fair, the other dark. Both intense, both gorgeous and interested in only me. How did I get so lucky?

After tonight, I would no longer be a virgin and I had no doubt they'd do a very thorough job of it.

"Red."

"Good girl."

"It is our goal to *never* have you say it, but while we've known you for a long time, we're moving into a space that you know nothing about. Yet. We may do things that surprise you, perhaps even scare you. So you have to use it. Promise us," Wilder said.

"If you don't, you'll get a nice red ass," King warned.

"I understand." I did. There'd been too much confusion so far. "I'll use it if you do something that is too much."

King looked to Wilder, who nodded, then slid to the side on the edge of the bed. Between one second and the next, I was rolled onto my stomach, bent at the waist so my knees were tucked beneath me, similar to Child's Pose in yoga. But when I did yoga, I wasn't bare from the waist up and I definitely didn't have two men touching me. My arms were out in front of me, my fingers gripping the blanket. I looked over my shoulder as King slid my braid to the side, then stroked down my back, over my ass to my thigh, then reversed direction, lifting my latex skirt along until it was flipped up about my waist.

I closed my eyes, took a deep breath. This was what I wanted...but it was intense. Ten minutes ago, I hadn't even known they wanted me...hadn't even known they were at Hawk's Landing and now I had my butt exposed. And soon—

"Now that is a pretty sight," King commented, his hand cupping my bottom. I felt a second hand, on the other cheek, and knew it was Wilder's.

"Pretty, but it could be prettier," Wilder said.

I gasped when his palm struck my bottom, the sound of it filling the room, the sharp sting making me gasp.

King spanked the other side and I wiggled my hips as the surprise of it, the slight burn, shifted to heat. God, that was so hot. I felt myself getting wetter just from that.

"There, now we've both got our marks on you. Bright pink handprints that claim you as ours," King said.

"We should take her downstairs and have her walk around and hold the back of her sexy skirt up so everyone can see our marks, know she belongs solely to us," Wilder added.

I whipped my head about to look at him, to see if he were serious. The idea was oddly exhilarating, to know I brandished a sign of their possession.

"Ah, princess, you like that idea," Wilder added as he looked into my eyes. One big hand went to my biceps, curled about it and helped me up.

"Stand before us," he added. He held me as I got my feet beneath me. While his eyes held mine, King's were on my body; my bare breasts, watched as the latex skirt fell down over my thighs covering me.

"Turn around."

Slowly, I faced away from them. My nipples hardened at the dark tone of his voice. While they were pushing me —god, this was so decadent doing as they said. It was all play now; it was sexy, but it wasn't sex. Only King's knuckles had grazed my nipples. They'd barely kissed me. I had a feeling they were getting me used to them, to doing as they said. Simple commands, nothing too dark or dirty. Yet. Still, they were definitely pushing me, testing me for what was to come.

"Lift the back of your skirt so we can see our claim on you."

I gripped the hem of my skirt in my fingers, curled it as I worked it up, higher and higher until it was bunched up in the back about my waist.

"Good girl," King praised. "Now go stand with your nose touching the wall, ass on display."

I paused, started to turn my head to question, but changed my mind. The cream-colored wall was a few feet in front of me. I went over to it, leaned forward slightly and touched my nose to it.

"You're not being punished, princess. Not this time. We're admiring our beautiful girl. The line of her back, the fullness of her breasts as they curve out, the narrow waist, gorgeous hips. Perfect ass and that little thong doing nothing to hide our handprints. Fuck."

Wilder went down the list as if describing a car he liked, but I didn't feel degraded. No, I felt special.

"If you keep us out again, Sarah, you'll have a *very* red ass and you'll stand in the corner with lots of time to think about things." King used my name, not princess. He was serious. Very serious. "Think of all the time we've wasted because none of us shared how we felt, what we all needed. We're committed to you, to this, but while you might submit, you're the one in charge."

"I understand," I murmured. I did. I had the power to stop it all. I could say red and all of this would be over. They'd wrap me in a blanket and hug me. Protect me. But no one would get what we all wanted.

So far, what we'd been doing was really hot. Heady. Sexy.

"Good girl. Now turn around and show us your sexy tits."

# 4

ARAH

KING'S VOICE had a smile in it and when I turned to look at him, I saw it. Yeah, he was smiling, but his gaze was squarely on my tits. Yes, tits. I'd never been into that word, thought it a little demeaning, but not now. Now, it sounded sexy and dirty. I bet I looked pretty dirty since I still held the back of my skirt up. I was covered in front, but that was the only place still unseen by them.

"Back on the bed. Same position as before."

I walked past them back to the bed, knowing they could see the way my breasts swayed as I moved. I wasn't small, anywhere. I shifted and wiggled, swayed and jiggled.

I let go of my skirt and crawled onto the soft mattress, dropped to my forearms.

"Reach back, bare that ass for us to see."

Shifting my weight to one arm, I did it. They could have done it for me in a matter of seconds, but they were patient as I revealed myself to them. Again, it was an opportunity for me to say red, to change my mind. To slow down or stop entirely.

No way. I was sooo green right now.

I exhaled, settled into position and was ready for whatever they would do next.

Their fingers hooked into the lacy edge of my thong and slowly tugged it down, but when it pulled away from my pussy, I felt it cling...cling, and then pull away.

"Look at that sticky honey," Wilder practically groaned as the damp scrap of lace settled about my knees. They shifted me to remove it entirely before the thong was dropped on the bed a few inches in front of my face. I couldn't miss the dark wet patch in the middle.

I felt the bed lift as they moved and when I tilted my head, I saw them standing to the side, arms folded, looking at me.

"Don't move, princess. We want to look our fill," Wilder said.

"You're gorgeous. We've dreamed about you like this," King added.

I could only imagine what I looked like, on all fours as I was. My ass was high, breasts hanging down, my nipples brushing the bed.

"We could walk up behind you, fuck you right now. Claim that cherry once and for all," King commented.

Wilder pulled out a cell, snapped a picture.

"Wilder...I don't want—"

"Shh," he said, putting one hand on the bed to lean close enough so I could see myself on the small screen. "Look at how we see you."

Yes, I was just as I described, every full curve on display. Lewdly, decadently. And more. Even the pink handprints were visible. They couldn't miss how wet and open my pussy was.

"So sexy, so submissive. I love how you remain in position even though you're nervous. Such a good princess."

I exhaled with his words.

"Now watch me delete this. You, like this, all bare and perfect, is just for me and King."

He pushed a few buttons and I watched as the picture was, in fact, deleted.

King went to the side of the bed and a growl escaped his chest. "Don't move from your position. Otherwise, you'll get your ass spanked some more."

I started to turn my head to see what he was doing, but Wilder came around to the far side of the bed, dropped to his knees so I could look right at him. His fingers pointed toward me, then his way. "Eyes on me. Don't close them, don't look away."

Okay. That shouldn't be too hard. But I felt something wet and soft slide along my pussy and I gasped, startled. A hand gripped my bare hip, held me in place.

Wilder's usually intense look softened, a small smile turned up at the corner of his mouth. "Like King's tongue? He's going to lick up all that sweet honey."

King's tongue? Oh. My. God. His mouth was on my pussy. They'd barely kissed me and this was what they started with? No, they'd started when Wilder carried me upstairs. If I'd wanted normal kisses, I'd have been fine with Danny Sayers from seventh grade.

"It is sweet," King said from between my thighs. I felt his warm breath...there. There! He could see *everything* up close and personal.

And taste. Oh god.

King. Had. His. Face. Between. My. Thighs.

I was on a bed, ass in the air, King licking me where no one had ever even seen before, Wilder watching my every expression. I whimpered.

"So fucking sweet. And she's dripping," King added as he licked me again.

"Eyes open, princess," Wilder warned.

Now I knew why he'd given me the warning earlier. It was almost impossible to look at Wilder with the things King was doing. His tongue circled my entrance, slid up a fold and to my clit.

I cried out his name.

"That's right, princess. Say my name," King said. It must have spurred him on, for his hands came to the backs of my thighs, his thumbs parting me so I was completely and totally at his mercy.

"Time to come for us, princess. I'm going to watch," Wilder vowed.

I'd made myself come many times. Hundreds, but it had never felt like this. Tingly and intense, hot and wet. Out of control. I could do nothing but take whatever King was going to give me and look into Wilder's dark eyes as I did so.

All I could do was submit.

My body did so readily; King was a voracious and thorough lover. Skilled, too, with the way he was getting me closer and closer to coming.

My fingers clenched the bedding, my back arched, pushing my hips into his face. My mouth fell open and my eyelids lowered halfway.

"I'm...oh god, I'm going to come!"

There was nothing stopping it. The way King gently yet ruthlessly licked my clit, then sucked it into his mouth was indescribable. But when he carefully slid his teeth over the sensitive nub, I was done for.

My eyes flared wide at the surprise of it, so much more intense than I'd ever imagined. My nipples were sensitive—I felt the rings rub and the blanket felt almost scratchy against the tender skin. Every inch of my body tensed as the heat, the bliss of it spread through me, like sweet poison through my veins.

"My turn," Wilder said, his voice harsh as he stood abruptly, stalked around the bed. I looked back and saw King move out of the way, wipe his mouth with the back of his hand.

Gripping my hips, he flipped me onto my back. Wilder put his hands on my knees, parted them and pushed them wide. I looked up at him as he stood over me. I'd never seen him look this way, almost feral. I could see the thick bulge of his cock in his jeans, pressing, I assumed painfully.

Wilder lowered himself and put his mouth on me, his broad shoulders keeping my thighs spread, my heels slid up and down his back.

Instantly, my fingers went to his hair, tugged. "Wilder!"

His hands settled on my breasts, cupped them, tugged on the nipples, gently twisted the rings as he ate me out.

I was ridiculously sensitive from King and Wilder easily pushed me to the brink and over the edge again. This pleasure was sweet and rolling, toe curling. Equally intense but...different. Just like the two men who gave them to me.

When he pushed up, he, too, wiped his glistening lips.

"Now that you're all warmed up, it's time to play," he said.

Neither man made any move to remove their clothes. While I was bare except for the skirt bunched about my waist and the heels, they had every piece of clothing on.

"Play?"

My inner walls clenched at the thought of what they had in mind next. Each of them took hold of an ankle, carefully undid the little clasps on the straps of my stiletto Mary Janes.

"See what makes you hot," King said, grinning as he slid the shoe off my foot, dropped it to the floor.

"I think you know the answer to that," I commented.

His eyes slid down my leg and right to my pussy.

"That's just one way," he replied.

"What about...what about you?" I asked, staring at the impressive erections thickly outlined in their jeans. Wilder's curved blatantly to the right and up toward his hip. King's also went to the right, but it went down the inside of his thigh, as if he had a baton in there.

"What are you trying to say, princess?" Wilder asked, glancing down at himself, then at me.

"Aren't you going to... get undressed? Let me touch you?"

Wilder quickly undid the buttons of his shirt, shucked it. Oh my. He had broad shoulders and a narrow waist. Dark hair on his chest looked soft as it narrowed to his navel, then to a thin line that disappeared into his pants. He kept his hands at his sides, let me look my fill.

Pushing up on my elbows, then all the way up, I knelt on the bed. He moved close so I could touch him, to feel the heat of his skin, feel the hard muscles beneath. God, it was better than I'd imagined.

Glancing up at him through my lashes, I caught him watching me.

"See something you like?" he asked, his voice rumbling.

I bit my lip. Nodded. Oh, yes. I absolutely did.

I'd thought of this, of what he'd look like, feel like, even smell like...for, well, forever.

King worked his blue shirt off, let it fall to the floor behind him, and I put a hand on him as well.

"Dark and light," I said dreamily to myself. "I get both of you."

And I was only reveling in their chests. There was so much more of them. While this wasn't bad, there were better...areas I wanted to see.

Reaching for their belt buckles, I hooked my fingers around the metal and pulled them both a touch closer. Of course, they let me tug them, otherwise it would have been impossible to do so.

As I began to fiddle with the belts, my fingers were only inches away from their bulging cocks, they stilled my motions.

"What?" I asked, looking up at them again.

"No dicks for you, princess."

I froze, my brain stalling on what Wilder said. "What?" I asked again. "I thought...I mean, if you're going to take my virginity then at least one dick is required."

I hadn't done it before, but I wasn't *that* clueless.

They both smiled. "True. Very true. But we're not claiming you until you've got our rings on your finger."

## 5

ING

WILDER AND I were the ones who were supposed to be on our knees, although we hadn't officially asked her to marry us. But the sight of her sated and naked—except for the skirt that was tangled up about her waist, made me just fine with this turn of events. I'd wanted to marry her for forever, known she was the one for me, the one Wilder and I would share together for as long as I could remember. But we'd had to wait. And wait. And wait for her. We'd gone about our lives, lived them. College, returning to run the ranch. For Wilder, college for him as well, but he'd gone into the Montana Fish and Game Department. We'd had girlfriends, women to fill the years while we waited for Sarah, but they'd just been fun. Nothing more.

With Sarah, there'd always been a connection. Her smiles lit up the room, that damn dimple destroying me, as she filled a place in my heart. I came alive when she was near. Her laugh, her kindness for others, her desire to lead a simple life as the Barlow librarian against her mother's wishes, especially with its meager salary. I loved that she lived her own life, not the one that bat-shit crazy woman planned for her involving marrying rich and frequently.

When Sarah's mother tried to bag me after her divorce from husband number three, I knew how special Sarah was. Fuck, to find the older woman in my bed had been a shitty surprise. I'd been twenty-three at the time and had a man's need to fuck, but not her. No fucking way. Not only because she was Sarah's mother, but I knew she was only naked and willing because I had a big ranch that had been handed down from generation to generation since the 1880s. The family land alone was valuable. The only ranch comparable in size to mine, to the Barlow land, was Steele Ranch.

I'd had no interest in becoming husband number four.

Besides, I'd been in love with Sarah even then, even then when she'd still been young. It sickened me to think what her mother had tried to do when all I wanted was sweet Sarah. Obviously, that incident had been kept top secret. Wilder knew, but it wasn't going anywhere else. Nothing had happened and Sarah's mom had left for California soon after.

Sarah had survived a ruthless, conniving role model

and had turned out completely the opposite. Thank fuck she'd used the example as what *not* to do.

She might have put on fet wear and wanted to check out a BDSM party, but our Sarah was a virgin. Sweet and pure, but with a very naughty, very kinky streak.

Yeah, she was fucking perfect for us.

Which meant our dicks stayed in our pants.

"You want to marry me?" she asked. Her dark eyes were wide, her mouth hanging open.

Yeah, we'd stunned her. She'd fucking stunned us by being here in black latex and a half-bra with pierced nipples exposed.

I shifted my cock in my pants just looking at the little gold rings that dangled from those gorgeous nipples. The idea of adorning them with little jeweled clamps, to see them sparkle, to dangle and swing as she moved made me hard as a rock. Fuck, little bells would be good. Hell, yes. She'd be naked in our house with little bells on those rings so we could hear her coming, to be a constant reminder of those fucking nipples.

Yes, I was obsessed with those big, thick nipples. Those full tits which were a hefty handful. And that bra that didn't do fucking shit except make my dick even harder... yeah, she'd be wearing a whole bunch of that lingerie, too.

Our girl liked kinky. We'd give her lots of kinky. No panties though. That thong we'd just stripped off her was the last pair she'd be wearing around us. I needed to know she was bare and dripping, ready for our dicks.

I growled and Sarah's eyes widened.

"You feel it too, don't you, princess?" I asked. "This

isn't just sex. Hell, it's always been more. For such a long time."

She dropped back onto her heels.

"Do you just want sex with us?" Wilder asked.

Her chin lifted and her eyes whipped to his. "What? No."

"Why is that?" he prodded.

"Because I can't just do...sex. I need more. A relationship. Affection. Love."

Inwardly, I sighed. That's right. Sarah had saved herself for us. She just hadn't said that specifically. Yet.

"Love," I repeated. "You won't have sex with someone without love."

She nodded.

"But you were just begging for our dicks, kneeling naked before us, undoing our belts."

Her cheeks flushed red at my words, crept down her long neck, over her chest and to the top swells of her breasts.

"I'm not a slut."

I dropped to my knees on the carpet so she was just a little taller than me. "Fuck no. But it's okay to share your sexuality, your passion, your desires with the men you love. And I mean *men*. Me and Wilder. Both of us. You love us both, don't you, princess?"

Wilder settled beside me so we were both on our knees before her as we should be. Her whiskey colored eyes were bright with unshed tears. She licked her lips, then nodded. "Yes. I...I tried not to, I really did."

I couldn't help but grin.

"Well, not very hard," she admitted. "But it's been so

long. I've wanted both of you and it was wrong, but I couldn't do anything about my heart. But I've known just as long that I need something more. I like kink."

My grin got even bigger.

"We do, too." I hooked my hand behind her neck, pulled her in for a kiss. It was supposed to be sweet and gentle, but it didn't work out that way. I plundered her with my tongue. Sank into her sweetness.

Finally, I lifted my head, licked my lips, tasted her still. "I may have pecked you on the mouth last summer, but that had been wrong. That hadn't been real. *This* was one hell of a first kiss."

She blushed. "We're doing all of this backwards. I mean, you've both...well, you know, tasted me in *other* places and we've barely kissed. We don't really know each other and you want to marry me."

I leaned back so Wilder could have his turn kissing her. "Princess, you think we don't really know each other? Lies get you spanked, you know."

"But...I don't know what kind of toothpaste you like or what side of the bed you sleep on or if you toss your clothes on the floor."

"That's all shit to work out when married. Why steal learning the good stuff for beforehand? Besides, you know all about us."

She arched one delicate dark brow.

"What am I allergic to?" Wilder asked her.

"Blueberries."

"What's my father's favorite sport to watch on TV?"

"The Little League World Series," she replied immediately.

It was true, his dad loved to watch the kids play baseball. He'd been the coach for Barlow little league and even the high school team before he retired with Wilder's mom to Florida.

"What's my favorite food?" I asked her.

She looked to me. "Spaghetti and meatballs."

I lifted my hand to my forehead. "How did I get this scar?"

"From your truck door."

There was a story there, but it wasn't worth repeating. But Sarah knew about it.

"See, you know us," I told her. "And we know you like Sweet Pea lotion, your favorite author is Jane Austen, you don't like corn on the cob and you never learned to knit, but your grandmother taught you how to crochet."

Her mouth fell open at my list of knowledge. "And you like things wild as fuck in the bedroom."

She paused and I could practically see the gears working in that smart mind of hers.

Slowly, she smiled. There, that look lit up the whole fucking room and made me want to spout about rainbows and fucking unicorns and shit.

"Yeah, I guess you're right. Not only about me being wild in the bedroom"—she glanced away at that—"but that we do know each other."

"That's right, princess," Wilder admitted. "We want all of you. But we won't take it without commitment. Real commitment. When you part those thighs for our dicks, you'll know you belong to us. You'll feel the weight of our rings on your finger, know that's the proof your pussy is ours. But not until then."

"Yes, I'll marry you," she replied. Her eyes widened as if her words surprised her.

Wilder kissed her, then I had my turn. Yeah, she was fucking sweet.

When I pulled back, she bit her lip, plump and red from our mouths on hers. "Does this mean we can't...do stuff until then?"

Wilder glanced at me. I could practically read his mind, but his words confirmed it. "Princess, we just licked your pussy. I'd say we can do stuff until we get you to the courthouse."

"Like what?" she breathed.

Wilder angled his chin. "Grab the headboard."

She stared at him for a moment as he stood, having to tilt her head back to keep eye contact, then crawled across the bed to do as he said. Obedient little submissive.

When she had her hands on top of the log-style headboard, she looked over her shoulder at us, then thrust her ass out. Her latex skirt had fallen down, but when she shifted, we could see a hint of our handprints still on her round cheeks, plus all that pink, wet pussy. And when I saw the little rosette of her ass wink at us, I had to palm my dick. Monday when the county courthouse opened was a long way off.

"Get that skirt off. I want to see every gorgeous inch of you," Wilder told her. She shimmied and shifted to get the garment off, then moved back into place.

"Here's what's going to happen now, princess," I said, standing as well. "We're going to see how many ways we can make you come without touching that pussy. Nothing goes near that cherry before our dicks on Monday. Your ass—because we're going to take you there, too—your mouth, your tits tonight are all fair game."

She glanced at us over her shoulder. Fuck, she was like a magazine centerfold, pink pussy peeking out, her nipples hard with the shiny rings. It was going to be hard not to come in my jeans. I wanted to pull my dick out and rub one out, to spurt my cum all over her pale skin. But no, that would wait until Monday. I'd save up all of it to fill that pussy instead. Nice and deep. So deep I didn't know where I ended and she began.

"Our wedding night, princess, you're going to have so much cum in that broken in pussy it'll be dripping out all week."

I watched as her eyes dilated at my dirty words. She really was a kinky girl. Yeah, she was absolutely fucking perfect.

Wilder went to the bedside drawer, pulled out a travel-sized bottle of lube, tossed it onto the bed. Yeah, we'd have to thank Matt and Ethan later for all the resort's amenities. "Reach back, princess, and grab that ass. Show us your tight little back hole. Time to see how many times you can come."

While she blushed hotly at Wilder's filthy words, she reached back and spread herself open for us, no questions asked, no safe word. I was done for. We might be in charge, but Sarah Gandry all but brought me to my knees.

## 6

ARAH

When Wilder and King dropped me off at my house the next day—King having driven my car since it had snowed during the night and I rode the two hours with Wilder—I dropped my overnight bag, leaned against my closed front door, slid to the floor. Grinned. I couldn't believe it. All of it. *Any* of it.

From seeing them at the resort to the wild and crazy night, to the rules they had put in place until they picked me up tomorrow for the courthouse wedding, it was insane.

I had on a pair of jeans and a black thermal shirt, King's hoodie sweatshirt over it, then my thick winter coat. But no panties.

After about the sixth orgasm, I'd fallen asleep, or

passed out, in Wilder's bed. While I'd been naked and tucked beneath the covers all night, King had returned to his room and Wilder had kept on his jeans and settled beneath the blanket. I had to assume that while they were adamant about not taking my virginity until we were married—married!—it wasn't easy for them to abstain. I'd seen the thick outlines, the solid bulges in their jeans which meant they were interested. Very interested. Very eager. The way they went at me...god. I got hot all over just thinking about it. I struggled to get out of my coat, let it fall to the floor beside me.

I tugged the front of King's sweatshirt up to my nose and breathed deep, took in his now familiar scent. I was going to marry them. Both of them! While I'd only legally be tied to one of them, I knew they both were going to be claiming me. And claim me they would, as soon as they got their rings on my finger. Until then, they'd certainly left their mark. Or marks. I knew there was a little hickey on the top of my right breast, just above the nipple. Wilder had left one on the inside of my thigh along with some whisker burn. And I had no doubt my butt was still red.

I was a little sore, a little tender in places like my nipples and my ass. And by ass I didn't mean my bottom, while that was a little tender and sore, too. They'd used the lube and their fingers to play there as I held on to the headboard. I'd lost my grip once as King slipped his thumb deep into my ass, slowly fucking me there as Wilder played with my clit. Each of them had had a hold of a nipple ring and gently twisted and tugged. I'd been completely and totally at their mercy, being pushed and prodded to orgasm after wild orgasm.

God, I'd been a total pleasure whore. They were *so* good at making me feel good, and they wouldn't let me reciprocate in any way. When I'd tried, trying to at least press my hand against them, they'd swatted my ass in playful punishment.

I rolled my eyes and shifted on the hard wood floor, remembering the way they'd knocked on my hotel room door this morning, entered, shut it behind me. Wilder had walked me back to my room to get dressed and packed up. When I let them in, they'd told me to pull down my pants to make sure I wasn't wearing any panties. And since I had been, they'd spun me about, bent me over my not-slept-in bed and spanked me. That hadn't been very playful. Not at all. After, they'd watched as I took the panties off and put my jeans back on. When they were finally satisfied and I had a very hot butt as a reminder of who was in charge of my pussy, we'd left for Barlow.

And now here I was, alone. Pantiless. I pushed off the floor, worked off my boots and left them on the mat by the door, dashed to the bathroom. I spun away from the mirror, pushed down my jeans, studied my bottom over my shoulder in the reflection. Yup, still red. A few distinct pink finger-shapes were still clear as well. This *sooo* wasn't me. I always wore underwear. Always did the right thing. Okay, perhaps except for the wild hair I'd had to get my nipples pierced, but other than that, I was a good girl. I followed the rules, was meticulous—a librarian had to be—and precise. I liked order, normalcy. Yeah, that had flown out the window last night. Along with my panties. I was officially a good girl no longer.

I grinned even wider, then let it slip. It fell away entirely.

They said we knew everything about each other. They were right, to a point. While we hadn't exactly been friends as I'd grown up, they'd always watched out for me. I'd see them and every time, their eyes had been on me. They'd come over and to say hi, check on me, specifically because of my mom. I'd always felt safe with them. Protected, even from afar. And now I could feel safe and protected up close.

But I had secrets, not like the fact that I had a very red, very spanked ass beneath my jeans. Big secrets. Nothing like the fact that I drank orange juice from the carton or always did my laundry on Sundays. That stuff they'd learn, just like Wilder had said, after we married.

But this biggie? They deserved to know.

My cell rang and I tugged up my jeans, ran to the entry where I'd dropped my purse. My heart galloped at the thought of it being King or Wilder. I had it bad, especially since they'd walked me to the door and left just a few minutes ago.

Shit. My mother. She'd already called several times this weekend, but I'd ignored them all. I had to answer this one or she'd never stop. I was alone and I could deal with her without the chance of getting King or Wilder involved. They knew she was difficult, but I'd hidden most of it from them. From everyone.

"Mother," I said.

"There you are. I've been trying to call you all

weekend." She sounded cranky, as usual.

I rolled my eyes, went into my small, tidy kitchen. "I've been busy."

"So disrespectful," she chided. "I was in labor for—"

"Thirty-six hours," I said, finishing her usual sentence, reminding me I'd been a burden for her since birth. I tugged open the fridge, rooted through the top shelf.

I heard her sniff through the phone, not because she was sad, but because she was mad. "Your brother doesn't ignore me."

*That's because he lives in your basement and mooches off of you for his lavish lifestyle instead of getting a job.*

"What did you call for, Mother?" I checked the date on a package of cream cheese, wrinkled my nose at it, then tossed it in the trash. I waited for her answer. For the matchmaking to begin. It happened every phone call.

"I met a man. Robert. He's a yacht salesman."

Oh brother. She'd divorced husband number five last summer and was now living in his Santa Barbara house she'd gotten in the settlement. Now, it seemed, she wanted a yacht. If she married the guy, she'd somehow get a one out of the arrangement. Not that she even liked the water. She got seasick looking at the Yellowstone River.

"That's nice," I replied neutrally, checking the dates on all my condiments. If I couldn't toss my mother out with the trash, the least I could do was empty my fridge.

"He has a son."

And there it was. A yacht salesman's son this time.

She didn't want the dad, she wanted *me* to have the son. For me to get her that boat.

Last week, it had been a new neighbor who'd retired at thirty from the film industry. Loaded. I paused, eyeing a jar of sundried tomatoes. "That's nice," I repeated. I knew better than to give her any kind of positive response. But now I had Wilder and King.

I huffed out a small laugh wondering how they would react to discovering my mother wanted me to marry a man in California. As alpha males, they'd go ape shit. And that had me smiling again. I liked the idea of them being all possessive with me. While they'd left me at my house, they hadn't been thrilled with it. But King had some chores to see to on the ranch, Wilder had paperwork to get done at the Fish and Game headquarters so they could have tomorrow free.

Our wedding day.

"—have dinner when you come to town next. Perhaps next week? Are you even listening to me, Sarah?"

"Sorry, I missed the last." Thinking of my men was much better than anything my mother had to say.

She harrumphed. "Since your father left you with nothing and as a silly librarian you're not living up to your potential, you could at least try to land a wealthy husband. I'll fly you in to meet Travis."

"Yeah, no thanks." I'd rather have my wisdom teeth pulled again than get on a plane to Santa Barbara for a blind double date with my mother and her yacht salesman potential-boyfriend.

"If not here in Santa Barbara, then there in Barlow,"

she continued, undeterred. "A rancher is always good. You always had your eye on Kingston Barlow. He'd be a good choice; the town's named after his family after all. Remember, land will hold its value until you can divorce."

Oh my god. She wanted me to marry a guy—King—with the intention of divorcing him and taking half his money. Just like she'd done with her long line of husbands. Over and over. If it worked for her, then she expected it would work for me. If she only knew I really *was* marrying Kingston Barlow she'd probably pee her pants. Or worse, fly here for the ceremony. I bit my lip.

"Your father—"

I cut her off. "Yes, I know about my father."

She sighed. "Aiden Steele never gave you the time of day."

True.

"He did give you child support," I countered.

My father had owned Steele Ranch until he died last year. My mother, who'd been born and raised in Dallas, had somehow ended up in Montana and gotten the man into bed, or at least the back seat of a car, to get pregnant with me. To trap him. From what my mother had always told me, he'd refused to marry her.

"Until you turned eighteen and then it stopped entirely," she snapped.

"Mother, I became an adult. Why should he support an adult?" I asked, defending him. I wasn't sure exactly why since he'd wanted nothing to do with me. While he hadn't shunned me outright, whenever I saw him in town —which had been very rarely—he'd given me a head nod as a way of greeting. Nothing else. Perhaps he'd thought I was like my mother.

But I'd begun to think otherwise when his lawyer had contacted me with the news Aiden Steel had put money into an account for me to pay for college. *Only* college, just in case I *was* like my mother and wanted a fancy car instead. Since I was of age, I hadn't had to tell her about it —she'd have wanted it for herself. When I'd told her I'd been accepted to the university in Bozeman, I'd only told her I'd gotten scholarship money and she'd sniffed at that instead of being proud.

"I was in college. It wasn't like you were taking care of me any longer."

"Still, he owed me."

"No, he didn't. He didn't owe you a thing."

"I raised you all those years."

"Mother, I'm not a pony you had to stable and feed. I am your daughter. You could have taken him to court."

"And what? Lost the child support? Please."

I looked up at my kitchen ceiling, then closed my eyes. That was my mother in one sentence. She'd raised me because of the child support money.

"I have to go," I told her, so done with this conversation.

"Let me know about the son because—"

I ended the call, dropped my phone on the counter. I put my hands on the edge, leaned against it. Breathed. I tried not to get riled up when she called, but it was impossible not to. She was my mother and that wasn't going to change. She was a money-grubbing schemer.

Since Aiden Steele had never put a ring on it, she'd

found a different rich landowner here in Barlow to bag instead. Husband number one. My half-brother, Karl, was the product of the marriage to husband number two, a lumber baron—that was what my mother had called him—from Seattle. That hadn't lasted long, only one summer—and long enough for her to get knocked up and get the quickie divorce. Aiden Steele had forced my mother's hand, making her come back to Barlow. No Barlow, no child support, which led me to believe he'd been somehow protecting me, at least keeping me nearby where he could keep an eye on me. While she'd never told me the amount, I'd always assumed it was large enough for her to force her stay in a small Montana town. And since she'd just validated in yet another phone call that I'd been worth keeping around for the monthly sum, it'd had to be pretty hefty.

Until it stopped when I turned eighteen. Thus, her new life in California where it never snowed. Since Karl had been only fourteen at the time, and was just like my mother—we'd never gotten along and I'd been thrilled to see him leave along with her—he'd learned from the expert to work his way through rich girlfriends to get by once he'd graduated high school. No college for him. Why would he do that when his career goals were to fuck and marry his way from one woman to the next to retirement?

As for Aiden Steele, he'd never publicly accepted me as his, but I didn't really care. My mother has always painted him a villain, but I figured while he might have been fooled for one wild night, he'd learned her true ways quick enough. Maybe I should have approached him and asked to live with him, but I figured if he had wanted me, he would have fought for me more.

No one knew I was his daughter. Aiden Steele hadn't shared it. My mother certainly hadn't. She wouldn't want to be considered a slut for having a child out of wedlock, especially back in the day. I rolled my eyes at the thought. I knew what everyone thought of her. A gold digger. Telling everyone my father was Aiden Steele wouldn't have changed anyone's opinions.

But now everything *had* changed. He was dead and he'd made me one of his heirs. My lawyer had died, but his son, Riley, had taken over. He'd notified me of Aiden Steele's death—not that I hadn't heard of it through the town grapevine by then—and told me of the will. Of the money and land I'd inherited.

But I'd made him keep the inheritance a secret, just like the college money. No one knew I was a Steele heiress and I hadn't touched a dime of the money. No one knew I was rich. Not my girlfriends, not even Wilder and King. If my mother got wind of it...

I slammed the fridge door closed, grabbed my phone. I was marrying Wilder and King tomorrow and I'd tell them about my father, about the inheritance before I did so, but I had to talk to my lawyer first.

"Riley, hey, it's Sarah Gandry. I'm sorry for calling on a Sunday, but can we meet? I have some news."

## 7

ILDER

"Princess, where are you?" I asked, leaning against the railing of Sarah's front porch. I could hear the tinge of panic in my words, but since she answered her cell, I knew she wasn't dead.

"On my way home now," she said, her voice clear through the phone. "Why?"

"Your car's in the driveway. We thought you were on the floor and injured or something."

"I got picked up." She paused. "You're at my house? Did I miss that you were coming over?"

While we'd made no plans today, I could barely get any of the paperwork I'd pushed off on Friday finished. I hadn't expected to run into Sarah and have my entire world change while I'd been away. Not that I minded.

Fuck, no. My dick was hard just thinking about what we'd done. How she'd responded. How she'd come. Again and again.

My mouth watered just remembering her sweet taste.

I'd half-assed my reports to get them finished, then texted King. He'd been right there with me, ready to see our girl again instead of waiting until morning. So when we pulled up to her house expecting her to be home, we'd both panicked. Her car *was* in the driveway and she wasn't answering her door. We'd rung the bell twice, even pounded. Nothing.

King had gone around the back, peeked into the back windows as I did the front. Nothing. She was a good girl and had most of her blinds closed—no fucker should be snooping about like we were—and everything was locked up tight. But that hadn't eased our minds. I'd envisioned her sprawled in her tub with a head injury or bleeding to death from a knife slice in the kitchen. Carbon monoxide. Spider bite. Every fucking possibility that could befall our girl.

Instead, I took a deep breath, turned rational and called her. I could've texted, but I wanted to hear her voice. To know someone hadn't kidnapped her and was texting for her. Yeah, I was fucking losing it.

"No, we hadn't made plans, but King and I have something for you and we decided to drop by."

"Oh, great." She sounded pleased. "I'll be there in a few minutes."

She hung up and I looked to King. He'd heard it all since I put it on speaker.

It was cold as fuck, even with the sun out. The snow sparkled and I pushed my sunglasses up my nose.

"We're going to have to get ourselves in check," King said, pacing on her front porch. I rubbed my hands together to warm them.

"No kidding. We're going to have to keep from panicking every time she leaves the house."

"Or our sight," he added.

I smiled. "Then we'll just have to keep her in bed, won't we?"

He grinned back. "Naked."

"There's two of us. She can have a dick in her at all times."

We grinned at the possibility—no, probability—and I adjusted myself in my jeans. Once we married her tomorrow, I had no intention of letting her out of bed, or off our dicks, for a long, long time. We had lost time to make up for.

A big truck pulled up in front of the house and Riley Townsend climbed out, went around the hood and opened the door for Sarah. She hopped down, saw us and smiled.

"Fuck, the dimple," King whispered.

Yeah, it was pretty fucking ruthless and she had no idea of its simple power.

Of hers.

She came up her shoveled walkway, her eyes on us the whole time.

"Hi," she said, her cheeks pink. While she seemed eager to see us, she looked...shy. Even after everything we'd done together, she was still innocent.

Barely. Only strong willpower and our jeans had kept us from claiming her the night before. And this morning.

"You know Riley, don't you?" she asked.

He stepped forward, shook my hand, then King's. "Of course. Been awhile."

He was a lawyer and a few years ahead of us in school. We'd played in a summer league softball team together a while back.

"Let's um...get out of the cold," Sarah prompted.

"I'll say goodbye then. They'll see you to the ranch, I assume," Riley said, glancing down at Sarah.

The ranch?

"Oh, um..." She flicked her gaze to us, then back at Riley. "Yes. I hope the addition of two more won't be a problem. Can I bring something?"

Riley grinned. "No problem at all. Kady and the other women are going to be thrilled. As for bringing something, just bring them." He pointed at us.

With a small wave, he turned and headed back to his truck, most likely eager to get back to the heater.

"Are we headed somewhere, princess?" I asked.

She gave a slight shiver, then pulled out her house key. We moved out of the way to let her open the door, then followed her inside.

She tugged off her boots and I stared at her ass in her jeans as she did so, remembering what it looked like bare and all pink from our palms.

"Want something to drink?" she asked as we toed off our boots in her wake.

"What's the matter?" King asked. "You look nervous."

She did. Her hands slid up and down her thighs, as if

they were damp with sweat. She bit her lip and her breathing was different. Definitely nervous. She couldn't hide anything from us.

She took a deep breath, let it out, then blurted, "Aiden Steele is my father."

What.

The.

Fuck?

Okay, I'd been wrong. She could definitely hide something from us.

"What?" King asked after a long, long pause as we processed her words.

She sighed, went into her small living room and paced, ran her hand over her hair. "I hadn't meant for it to come out like that, but you guys have this death stare thing going on and I can't *not* tell you things when you look at me like that."

We followed her into the room, but we remained just inside the doorway.

"That's good to remember, but you missed the important part," King continued.

She turned and looked up at us. Tilting up her chin, she said, "Aiden Steele is my father."

Yeah, that was what she'd said the first time.

"How long have you known this?" I asked.

"All my life."

All her life?

"Your mother—"

"Yeah, she's my mother all right," she grumbled. "You're well aware she likes to collect rich husbands. I guess Aiden Steele was her target about twenty-four years ago. While she hasn't admitted this, I'm thinking she tried to trap him, but he never took the bait."

"And Riley's your lawyer," I said, putting some of the pieces together. I was friendly with Townsend, but not close. Knew he was a lawyer, even knew he was the executor of the Steele estate. Hell, everyone in town knew it. I worked with Archer Wade, the town sheriff, and he'd told me he'd fallen for Cricket, one of the daughters who'd come to Barlow because of the inheritance.

I didn't know too much about Aiden Steele. I'd seen him in town a few times over the years, but we'd never spoken. From the Barlow gossip mill, I knew he'd never married and up until he died, no one knew of any kids to inherit his ranch. It had been a Steele property for generations. But that same gossip mill had tons of fodder after his death when it was discovered he had five daughters to whom he'd left the ranch. Three of them had been found. Riley, along with Cord Connolly, had married the first heiress to arrive. Kady.

I didn't remember her maiden name, but I knew she'd married them. Yup, both of them. She was also *very* pregnant with their first child. The other two women, Penny and Cricket, had also come to Barlow last summer. I'd met Penny once as she'd married Jamison, who was the foreman at Steele Ranch, and Boone. As for Cricket, we'd yet to meet, but she'd hooked up with three guys—one of them being Archer—and lived on the ranch.

Maybe claiming Sarah together wasn't as rare as we'd first thought, especially now that she was a Steele. No, she'd always been a Steele.

"How come he didn't claim you as his daughter? I

mean, you lived in the same town," King asked, his hand rubbing the back of his neck. "You're not bothered by that?"

Yeah, this was heavy shit.

She shrugged. "I always knew who he was to me. My mother never hesitated to bash him, but she did it quietly, at home. She still does," she grumbled. "She didn't want anyone to know. Whatever." She rolled her eyes. "He paid child support, gave me money for college. I think he did all he could."

"He could have loved you," King tossed back. While his parents were dead now, they'd loved him. No doubt about it. When he had kids—no, when *we* had kids with Sarah—he'd be as hands-on as his dad had been.

"True, but I don't know if he was capable of it. I mean, he had *five* daughters. Claimed none of them until he died. I think the money for college was proof he cared about me in his own way. I'm fine. Really," she added. She looked okay, but shit like this could fester. And since her mother was a bitch, I was still surprised she didn't need counseling.

I was mad. Really mad. How could a father not want Sarah?

"I'm angry for you then," I told her.

She came up to me, lifted her hand and cupped my jaw. "I love that about you." Her tongue flicked out, licked her lips. "I love *you*."

Those words. Fuck. I'd been hoping to hear those from her for years.

"Don't distract me from wanting to kill your father."

She smiled and that dimple popped out. "Good thing

he's already dead. I'm sure there's a big line ahead of you anyway. I mean, Kady, Penny and Cricket all have men who probably hate Aiden Steele, too, for the same reason."

"Yeah, but from what I hear, they never met him, never knew he even existed," King added. He was pissed, too.

"Why didn't you tell us sooner?" I asked.

"Because until last night, I didn't think things were going to work between us."

"And now?" King asked. "Legally, you're marrying me tomorrow at the courthouse. You'll be Wilder's too, but you'll get my name. Our kids will inherit the Barlow Ranch."

"And part of the Steele Ranch, it seems," I added, thinking of the huge ranch outside of town. It's only rival for size was King's. "That's why you were talking to Riley?"

She cocked her head to the side. "Sort of. I'm going to get a Coke. You guys want one?" she asked, walking into the kitchen.

We followed.

"Princess," I prodded as she took a can from the fridge.

"When I was younger, I kept who my father was a secret because of my mother. *She'd* made it a secret and it was difficult enough dealing with her." She held out a second can and I took it from her, wanting to do something with my hands other than making a fist. I hated her mother.

"I really dislike your mother," King said, voicing my

thoughts, skipping the word *hate,* although I knew that's what he wanted to say.

He shook his head when offered a can of his own.

I popped the top, took a swig.

Sarah closed the fridge, moved to her small dining table set in front of a bay window that overlooked her snow-covered backyard. "When I was older, I kept it a secret because, well, I thought I owed it to my father. He paid for all of my college, housing, books. All of it so I didn't have to work at the same time. Since he hadn't told anyone about me, I chose to do the same about him."

"You mean he paid for your silence," King added, dropping into the chair across from her, his long legs sticking out across the wood floor.

I leaned against the counter, set the can down and crossed my arms over my chest.

She shook her head. "He paid for my college—not that my mother knows that. He lived a year past that. Let it go. That's not the point here."

King pinched his lips together when he realized she wasn't going to budge. She might not hate him, but we could.

"Even after, what, seven or eight months, I haven't told my mother that I inherited. She thinks I didn't get a dime and I want it to stay that way. The minute she heard he died, she called me. Asked if I'd inherited the ranch since I was his daughter, that it was owed to me. At the time, she didn't know about the other sisters, no one did. She started making all kinds of plans about the main house, what she was going to do to it, the furniture she was going to buy, how she was going to sell all the animals and then talk with a developer to build a golf course or something."

Oh shit.

"I lied. I told her I hadn't even been named in the will. Riley is the executor of the estate and I asked him to keep me a secret. Since he's my lawyer, he has followed my wishes. While people know now there are five daughters, no one knows one of them is me. Until now, until you."

She took a sip of her drink, used the back of her hand to wipe her mouth. So unladylike, but I doubted she even knew she'd done it.

"Riley has helped me set up a trust for the money so it's not obvious that it's mine. But now, I guess it will be out there."

"Why?" King asked.

"Because I'm marrying you."

"That's right, you are," he said, taking her hand in his, kissing the knuckles in a remarkably gentle gesture. "But that doesn't change a thing. I don't give a shit about that money. If you want Riley to write something up, a pre-nup or whatever that's fine, but he better do it tonight because you'll be legally mine come morning."

"And mine," I added. "I don't have a ranch to give my wife like King does."

I didn't. My dad was a dentist and my mom was a homemaker. While they weren't rich, they'd certainly never hurt for money. I'd had everything I could have ever wanted growing up. The important stuff like family. Love. The safety of belonging. Sarah never had that.

Sarah stood and came over to me, wrapped her arms about me. I pulled her close, put my chin on the top of her head. "I don't want to be rich," she told me. "I never did. I like this house, my quiet life. I knew going in that a library science degree wasn't going to make me lots of money."

"A quiet life we can give you. As for this house? We won't all fit. We'll live at King's ranch if that suits you. Lots of room for a family."

She tilted her head up, smiled. "All right."

I kissed her. There was no way I could resist. She tasted sweet like her drink and beneath, just like her.

"Where are you taking us later, princess?" I murmured, staring into her dark eyes, which were now hazy with need from the kiss. "Riley mentioned you bringing us with you somewhere."

"To Steele Ranch. Sunday dinner."

King stood, turned Sarah to face him, cupped her jaw with his hand. "I thought you wanted it to remain a secret."

"The trust is in place. That's all set so my inheritance isn't in my name. I've also had Riley list you both as beneficiaries, that way if something happened to me, it wouldn't go to my mother. That's what he drew up today because it would've otherwise. While I don't know my half-sisters really at all, they're probably really nice and I don't want them to be stuck with my mother."

I hated the idea of something happening to her, to have her even talk about that kind of eventuality, but she was smart. Realistic. Without stating a beneficiary or leaving a will stating otherwise, her mother would get Sarah's estate, and that included one-fifth of Steele Ranch. And since we'd sprung the marriage thing on her last night, no wonder she'd had to rush and meet with Riley today.

"We don't want your money, princess," I said, making sure she understood. "We only want you."

"That's right," King confirmed.

She smiled sweetly. "I know, but tomorrow you're going to be my husbands. What's mine will be yours, and I really don't want any of it being my mother's."

"Fuck, princess. I love you," I growled, kissing her again. She was so unlike her mother. She didn't have a selfish bone in her body.

When I let her up for air, she said, "I had to tell you about my father, about Steele Ranch before we married. A wedding meant the three of us would become a family and I realized I already had some. Kady, Penny and Cricket are my sisters and I've avoided them because of this secret. Really, because of my mother. I don't want to miss out any longer."

King pulled her up so she went on her tiptoes and he kissed her, too. Open mouthed. A touch desperately, as if we hadn't kissed her or spanked her ass this morning.

When he pulled away, she was breathing hard, her cheeks were pink, this time definitely because of us.

"You said you had something for me?" she asked, her eyes excited for the idea of a gift.

King grinned. "You'll never guess this present."

"Jewelry?"

King's pale eyes met mine. I shrugged. "You tell her."

"You're good, princess. Definitely jewelry. And you're going to be gorgeous wearing it."

## 8

ARAH

"This isn't the jewelry I had in mind," I said, glancing down at the reflection of my bare breasts in the mirror over my dresser. Dangling from each of the little gold hoops was a blood red stone. They were big, about a half an inch long and weren't too heavy, but since I wasn't used to any kind of weight, I definitely felt them. When I moved, they swung about, bumping into my skin.

"Oh, it's definitely something we had in mind," King said, staring, his usually pale eyes were dark and stormy. He liked what he saw.

When I glanced at Wilder, he, too, practically drooled at the sight of the gems.

"We're not done, princess," Wilder said, the dark glint in his gaze a sign that they were switching from eager men adorning their future wife to doms doing as they wished to their sub.

"Oh?" What else could there be? I couldn't take any more weight on my nipples until I got used to it. As it was, they tingled, the constant slight tug went right to my clit and made me ache, made my inner walls clench.

Wilder stuck his hand in the bag King had gone to retrieve from his truck. Wilder had said that while he'd gotten some paperwork done at the Fish and Game office, he'd also taken the time today to stop by the adult store to pick up some...jewelry.

My eyes widened and I spun about to face him. I gasped at the feel of the gems swinging wildly, pulling on my nipples. I took a breath, let the tingles subside. "That's huge!"

It was a metal butt plug with a jeweled base the same color as the nipple gems.

Wilder winked at me. "It's the beginner size. Trust me, our dicks are much bigger than this. We'll get you ready for them."

The idea of them fucking me there, just like they had with their fingers the night before, had me clenching again. Whimpering.

"Tug down those jeans, princess, and let's get you all decorated," King said, leaning against the door to my closet. The bedroom wasn't big and with the two of them looming, it felt tiny. I felt tiny, too.

They stared at me, waiting. Wilder held up the plug, King grabbed a small bottle of lube from the bag. God, I hoped there wasn't much else in there. But this was my choice. All of it. Well, they were going to marry me even if

I didn't want a plug in my butt. I could say red and they'd respect that, perhaps just use their fingers and play like they had the night before. That would be the tame thing to do—in comparison. But did I want that? Hell, no. I didn't want tame. I never had.

And the plug? It was big...to me, and I wasn't quite sure how it was going to fit, but their dicks *were* bigger. I could tell from the impressive bulges that were obvious even now. They'd told me last night how they would eventually fuck me at the same time, one in my pussy, the other in my ass. They'd begun those preparations last night, ass training as they called it. The term was a little mortifying, but it had been fun. Besides, they wouldn't push me past what I could take. And they'd only given me pleasure, and a spanking, which I'd never tell them I liked.

I took a deep breath, undid my jeans, pushed them down and over my hips.

"Turn around," King said, his voice in that deep tone that had goose bumps rising on my arms. I complied. "Hands on the dresser. Good girl. Now down on your forearms. Yes, like that."

I moved as he wanted, settling so I was leaning down, my butt out.

"Arch your back and show us that gorgeous ass," Wilder added. "Fuck, princess, look how pretty those nipples look with the gems tugging them down."

I felt how they were being pulled and that made me wet, which they'd be able to see in a matter of seconds.

Curving my spine, my butt thrust out. I'd always thought that part of me was too big since I'd always been considered the short and curvy girl, but the way King and Wilder grasped it, spanked it, stared at it, played with it, they liked it just fine.

I gasped when a cool drizzle of the lube slid down over me.

"Deep breath, princess," Wilder said. Both men were behind me and I watched them in the mirror. I felt the cold press of the plug as it was worked in. Their gazes were on me there as the object was slowly pushed in. I squeaked when the broadest part stretched me wide, then it slid into place with a slick and silent plop.

"There," Wilder said. "Gorgeous."

King grabbed my arm and helped me stand, but with my pants just above my knees, I was a little off balance. He dropped down to his haunches. "Let's get these off of you."

I mechanically lifted one leg, then the other to help him. "We're going to Steele Ranch soon."

"That's right. You'll wear all your pretty jewelry to the dinner."

I froze. "What? I can't do that!"

King turned me about and his face was right in line with my pussy. "Yes, you can. And you will."

"You aren't serious," I countered.

"Very," Wilder added as he came back from washing his hands in my bathroom. "You can say your safe word if you want." He arched a brow.

I wasn't hurting. I wasn't *really* uncomfortable. It felt weird. Awkward. Full. And the nipple gems only made a constant pull which set my arousal to a simmer. And they knew that.

"No, I'm okay."

"Then you'll do what pleases your men."

"I need clothes at least," I argued. That was where I drew the line, where they *would* hear me say red.

King kissed the bare skin just above my trim landing strip, then stood.

"Princess, no man will see you like this. That pretty jewelry's just for us. Go find a skirt or dress to wear. Jeans aren't going to be that comfortable with the plug and you'll get a big wet spot from the way your pussy's dripping."

Duh. And god, I should be mortified, but King's words just made me so dang hot. And wetter. Yeah, a skirt was definitely required.

With a little swat to my bare butt, they urged me toward my closet to find something that would work with gems in my nipples and a plug in my ass. Yeah, meeting my three half-sisters for the first time was going to be great.

KING

"HOW ARE YOU HOLDING UP?" I asked Sarah, pulling her into me for a hug. I kissed the top of her head, smelled her fruity shampoo. Felt the hard press of the gems dangling from her nipples against my chest.

She'd had an intense dinner, although everyone had

been great. Riley had told everyone to expect us, but not why. He'd been the secretive lawyer to the very end.

But that meant Sarah had been the center of attention. Telling three women they were her half-sisters had been hard, especially since they'd all lived in the same town for six months or more, seen her around, even talked with her at the library while she'd kept the secret.

They hadn't been mad and had understood, especially since most of the guys knew of her mother from growing up. They'd remained quiet as if they took the saying, *if you don't have anything nice to say, don't say anything at all* to heart.

I had a feeling I wasn't the only guy Sarah's mother may have hit on. As far as bank accounts went, I might have owned a big homestead, land that went back in my family to the 1800s and was worth a ton, but Lee was a professional rodeo rider and he probably raked in the cash from his winnings. Cord had his own investigations business and the others...well, we all worked hard. None of the Steele women would want for anything, that was for damned sure.

"Okay," she said, wrapping her arms about me. We were in the great room of the Steele Ranch main house, although I'd pulled her off to the side. On the couch was her very pregnant sister, Kady, and her other very pregnant sister, Penny. Both of them looked as if they'd each swallowed a basketball. Only seven months along, to me, they looked ready to pop.

The idea of getting Sarah pregnant had my cock stirring in my pants. To know that the baby growing within her was something we'd made together along with Wilder was arousing and awoke my inner Neanderthal. But we had yet to mention kids. Once we got our rings on her finger in the morning, we could talk about it all she wanted. And if a baby was what she desired, we'd sure as hell put all the effort into making that happen.

"Overwhelmed," she added.

"I thought you'd be nervous," I said.

She tilted her head up to look at me and whispered, "How can I be nervous when all I can think about is the plug in my ass?"

I stifled a groan. Wilder, who'd grabbed a brownie from a plate on the large coffee table, glanced our way. I gave a slight head shake and he popped the dessert in his mouth, then went to join Cord and Archer, who seemed to be adamantly talking about bow hunting, based on their hand gestures.

Cricket sat on Sutton's lap while her other two men flanked her, all of them taking the large couch across from Kady and Penny. Cricket laughed at something Penny said. The petite blonde had her hand resting on her huge belly, Boone had his hand on the back of her neck, massaging it.

"Don't worry, we'll take care of you when we get home. If you need to come sooner, just let us know and we'll take you to an empty room and eat you out until you come. You know how much we like to eat pussy."

She whimpered and all heads turned her way. Fortunately, her body was blocking the way my dick was hardening into a steel pipe from that sound alone.

"Sarah, I can't believe you were going to get married

tomorrow without any bridesmaids," Kady said. "Now we all get to join you."

Of the three sisters, Kady was the bossy one. Perhaps it was because she was a teacher who she was able to herd people better than any sheep dog. While Cricket had been on her own pretty much all her life and had graduated in December with a degree in nursing, she was the quiet one. At least in comparison. Penny was the mild one, although she also seemed to be the most visibly voracious for her men. I hadn't missed the way Boone had dragged her off somewhere just before dinner and she'd returned with the large flannel shirt she wore buttoned incorrectly and a very satisfied smile on her face.

No one had commented, except for Kady who'd teased her sister for her ability to come so quickly.

"Oh, um, okay," Sarah said. While she'd had a younger brother, they hadn't been close. She'd pretty much raised herself. Thankfully, she'd turned out nothing like her crazy mother. But that didn't mean Sarah wasn't overwhelmed by all that had happened to her in a matter of twenty-four hours.

It was time to pull a Boone move, especially since I couldn't do anything with a pipe in my pants.

I took her hand. "Excuse us," I said to the room at large, and dragged Sarah down the hallway. I peeked in one door, found a powder room, then continued on. In the back of the house, I found the laundry room. It was big, with plenty of counter space and storage. A small window looked out over the prairie. Neat as a pin. Either Cricket and her men had OCD or there was another laundry room in the house. For what I wanted to do, the space was perfect. And private.

I shut the door behind me.

"King, what are we doing in here?" she asked, looking around.

"I want my dessert."

She frowned and when I dropped to my knees before her, her eyes widened. "Here? Now? What about Wilder?"

I grinned as my hands slid up her legs, clad in black tights. "Here. Now. Wilder can have his turn later. We won't always take you together, princess. Sometimes you'll be all mine, like now, sometimes you'll get a good fuck from Wilder. Sometimes we'll claim you together. We'll have our own bedrooms and share you."

"Oh," she whispered, understanding a little more of how it would be starting tomorrow.

"I can't wait until we get you home to get my mouth on you. I love you. I love to eat your pussy. Wet for me?"

I had no doubt she was, but I loved to see the way her cheeks turned pink at the question, the way she nodded shyly. We'd already done all kinds of dirty, filthy things to her, but she was still a virgin.

"What will everyone think?" she whispered, as if they could hear her. They might when she screamed her pleasure in a minute.

"They'll think you're taken care of by your men." I slid my hands up over her knees, higher still and found the edge of her thigh-high tights. The sight of the thick wool in contrast to the pale, supple skin of her inner thighs had me rushing. I wanted her. Bad.

"Hold up your skirt. Higher. Yes, like that. Good girl,"

I praised when she had the material bunched up about her waist. Beneath, she wore black thigh highs and nothing else. Her pussy was bare. When I slid my hands around and cupped her ass, I felt the jeweled base of the plug with the tips of my fingers.

"Such a good girl," I repeated. "So wet. All because of the plug, isn't it? Have you thought of anything but having your ass filled nice and deep? That it pleases us?"

I didn't let her answer, instead, put my mouth on her. Lapped all that need right up. Her taste, so sweet, coated my tongue. Her scent, ripe and tangy, filled my senses. And all that sticky wetness, covered my mouth and chin.

Her hands went to my hair as she kept a hold on the skirt, the dark fabric over my head. Her fingers tangled in my hair as I found her clit and worked her to orgasm in a matter of seconds. My girl was well primed and ready to go. When she came, she dripped all over me and I licked it all up. Fuck, yes.

The door opened and Sarah startled, her fingers tightening in my hair, but I wasn't worried. I knew it was Wilder. If it were anyone but him, they'd have knocked, especially since coming down the back hallway they would have heard her come and know we needed some privacy. She was completely covered, the skirt above me and even then my face shielded her pussy. All they'd get a glimpse of was me on my knees and between her parted thighs.

I sat back on my heels, wiped my mouth with the back of my hand. Sarah instantly pressed her skirt down, even though Wilder had seen everything she had to offer. Up close.

"My turn." Wilder pressed his palm against his cock through his jeans.

I knew how he felt. My balls ached with the need to sink into that pussy, to get coated in all that sticky honey. Tomorrow. *Tomorrow.*

I stood, kissed Sarah once more, then left. When I pulled the door shut behind me, Wilder's words followed me out. "Turn around and lift up that skirt, princess. Show me your pretty jewelry."

I grinned as I ducked into the powder room and cleaned up, and had to think of baseball and deworming cattle to get my dick to go down enough so I could rejoin the others.

Tomorrow couldn't come soon enough. Sarah better get enough time with her sisters tonight because she wasn't going to see them, or anyone, for a while once we said our vows.

 ARAH

"OMG, what did they do to you in there? You look like you need a nap," Kady said, pulling me into the kitchen.

One of the men came into the room, but she gave him a dirty look and he turned around and left. I wasn't sure who it was. I was too out of it to pay him much attention.

"Sarah?" Penny asked.

All three of my sisters stood in front of me, staring. Kady's and Penny's bellies stuck out and helped give me some room. They were huggers and close-talkers, two things I wasn't used to.

"I'm fine," I replied.

They all grinned. "Yeah, we can see that," Cricket said. "I guess the sex is pretty good."

"All Barlow men are skilled," Kady commented, glancing at Cricket.

"You've had sex with a bunch of Barlow men?" Penny countered.

"Two. Don't forget, little sister, that Boone just dragged you off not an hour ago," Kady said, her voice sassy. "Between the four of us, we've claimed nine men from Barlow. I'd say that's a pretty good number."

"We didn't have sex." The words slipped out and they all stared at me, wide eyed. I hoped my clothing was all set to rights. Wilder had removed the gems from my nipple rings and the plug from my ass—using the sink in the laundry room to clean it before sticking it in his shirt pocket. I felt empty now, my bottom a little tender from stretching around the plug. It made me wonder what it would feel like with their cocks finally fucking my pussy. Would I feel full like I had with the plug? Did it burn and ache the same? Would their cocks be too much? Would they fit?

I glanced into the other room and eyed Wilder who stood by the fireplace. Yes, he was drinking coffee and talking with Cord with a butt plug tucked into his shirt pocket. While I couldn't see the usual thick bulge of his cock that angled up toward his hip right now, I knew it was there, knew it was big. Really big. I clenched down on nothing, my thighs slippery as I rubbed them together. My clit tingled with the need to come. Again.

Wilder and King made me completely insatiable, and we hadn't even fucked.

"You didn't have sex and you still look like you had a whole bunch of orgasms?" Penny asked. "Jamison is like that. Boone likes sex, likes to see how fast he can get me to come on his dick, but Jamison likes to play. To warm me up, he says, for when we get home."

She looked at me dreamily, as if she couldn't wait to get home right now.

Cricket angled her head toward Penny. "This, including the bold words, all coming from the virgin of the group. Obviously, not any longer." Cricket put a hand on Penny's belly.

I gave a slight laugh. "I guess that's me now."

"You're...no way." Kady shook her head, clearly not believing me. She put a hand on her hip as if to ease the pregnancy discomfort. "You guys have known each other forever. No way you just got together out of the blue and are getting married."

"You don't believe us?" We'd told everyone that we'd dated in the past but the timing hadn't been right, until now. Now we were finally getting married. No one needed to know we were into kink or that we met by chance because of the BDSM party at Hawk's Landing.

Kady's mouth fell open.

"Of course she's telling the truth," Penny said. "Why would she lie?"

I felt weird, standing in the middle of the kitchen with the three of them practically in my face and grilling me. They weren't being mean, but inquisitive, how I assumed sisters were supposed to be.

"Can I get some coffee?" I asked, deflecting.

Penny, who seemed to be a people pleaser more than the others, went to get me a mug. Kady eyed me, trying to decide if I'd lied or not. Cricket just shook her head and rolled her eyes.

"I've been in love with Wilder and King for years. Since I was thirteen. That's really weird, being so young and all, so I just let it alone until we dated last summer." I shrugged. "It didn't really work out, but I saw them again last night. Things just...clicked. Still, it's crazy to get engaged after less than twenty-four hours."

"Crazy? We're all crazy," Penny said, pointing her finger between the three of them. "Cricket had a one-night-stand which turned into a weekend with three guys, one of them ending up being Sutton who worked here at Steele Ranch which she coincidentally inherited. Kady slept with her men within hours of arriving in Montana."

"On the front porch," Kady added, clearly proud of that.

"And I dropped my virginity like a prom dress," Penny offered. "Trust me, you're a Steele sister."

"You could have told us who you were and we'd have kept it a secret," Kady said.

"Ha!" Cricket and Penny both shouted at the same time, as if that would have been impossible.

Penny looked to me. "Whatever the start with Wilder and King, now you're getting married. It's really romantic," she said, handing me a steaming mug. I was glad she changed the subject. "Sugar or milk?"

"Milk, please."

"I'll get it," Cricket said. "Go lean against the counter or something before Jamison comes in and makes you go sit down." She pointed at Kady. "You, too.

I swear, overprotective men are why I'm staying on the pill."

Knowing she was right, Kady and Penny went to get stools from the kitchen's peninsula and sat down, leaning their elbows back on the counter behind them to give their bellies room.

Cricket brought me a small carton of milk and I poured some into my mug, then handed it back.

"You two must have gotten pregnant right away," I guessed since they'd only come to Barlow last summer.

"Pretty fast," Kady said.

"The first time," Penny shared.

The first time. That would be tomorrow for me. Good thing I had an IUD or I'd probably be pregnant right away myself. No doubt Wilder and King would be virile and attentive. And since King had said they were going to fill me with so much cum it would drip out of me all week, they'd ensure it happened.

"I'm impressed you've saved yourself for marriage. It's going to make tomorrow really special," Penny said.

"You got married right away, too?" I asked, seeing the beautiful ring on her finger.

She smiled. "Oh no. Long story, but I had lost my virginity the first night we got together. But I'd saved myself, although it wasn't like I knew them all my life like you and Wilder and King. It just worked out that way. I'm glad now."

I nodded, understanding. "Exactly. There just hasn't been anyone I've wanted besides Wilder and King. So it never happened." I left out that I liked kink, liked submission. They might know I got off in the laundry room, but the butt plug, the spankings weren't being shared. "And it's not me who wants to wait to have sex. It's them. I had my hands on their belt buckles, eager, but they refuse to take their pants off until I'm theirs." I held up my left hand, wiggled my bare ring finger.

King came in, grabbed my coffee and took a sip. "Everything okay?" he asked, his blue eyes studying me closely.

I bit my lip, nodded. He kissed my forehead, then left.

We burst out laughing.

"I can only imagine what's beneath those pants," Cricket said, her eyes alight with humor.

Penny smacked her arm. "Says the woman who has three dicks of her own."

We stared at Penny for a second, then started laughing again.

I'd missed out on this. On sisters. It was pretty amazing. And now I had them, plus Wilder and King. It couldn't get much better...unless I could get in their pants.

---

WILDER

"THAT WAS QUICK," Sarah said as I gripped her waist and lifted her up and into King's truck.

We were in the parking lot of the Barlow County Courthouse, the old turn-of-the-century brick building behind us. King had the marriage license in hand, his and Sarah's signatures as husband and wife, mine as one of the witnesses.

King had folded the center console up so she could sit between us. No fucking way would she sit in the back. I wanted to be as close to her as possible. I climbed into the seat beside her. Her sisters and their men had come to witness, but had left, knowing we wanted to get Sarah home and alone. And naked.

"Clearly the judge knew he needed to give the short version of the wedding vows," King said, sliding in behind the wheel. He winked. "Mrs. Barlow."

Fuck, the sound of Sarah having King's name made my dick hard. It was official.

We'd arrived at exactly nine o'clock, neither of us wanting to wait a second longer than necessary to make her ours. If only yesterday hadn't been Sunday and the courthouse closed, she would have already been ours. I lifted her left hand, saw the simple gold band King had put on her finger with his vows. Reaching in my pocket, I pulled out my ring for her. Held it up. I wanted to make it official between us, too.

Sarah's eyes flicked up to mine. She licked her lips, which were shiny with some kind of girlie gloss. Besides that, she had on a touch of makeup. Something dark and smoky that brought out her whiskey colored eyes, her full brows. Thick lashes. And those lips...fuck.

"With this ring, I thee wed," I said, my voice deep. Clear. It didn't matter we were in King's truck as I said these precious words. As long as I was with her, that I was getting my ring on her finger, was all that mattered. "To have and to hold from this day forward until death do us part."

Tears filled her eyes, slid down her cheeks as I slipped my silver band on her finger to join King's. Side by side, they looked perfect.

"I love you, Wilder," she whispered.

"I love you, too," I growled. Glancing around, I knew this wasn't the place to kiss my bride. Not when she'd just married King. "Now that we're hitched, let's get our wife home. I want to kiss her properly. I've been waiting years for this."

King started the engine, grinning. Yeah, he felt it too. We had our girl. Between us all legal-like. Nothing would tear us apart now. And soon, we'd claim all of her. Every sweet, hot inch of her.

The ride to the Barlow Ranch usually took thirty minutes. We made it in twenty. And upstairs to King's bedroom in another minute.

When he kicked the door shut behind him, I exhaled. This was it. The moment. Her rings glinted on her finger from the bright sunshine through the window. The bed was big enough for all three of us, at least to fuck. We were alone. Hell, no one was around for miles. Sarah wouldn't have to stifle any sounds of pleasure. We'd hear her come, hear her as we took her for the first time. She wouldn't have to hold anything back. Ever again.

And it started right now.

I glanced to King and he nodded. While Sarah looked nervous, she also seemed excited. Her body twitched with adrenaline, with need. Her eyes were almost black and her nipples were hard though her pretty white dress. We'd ditched our coats by the front door.

It wasn't a bridal gown, but it was perfect. With the halter top, it made it easy for King to undo the bow at the nape of her neck, let the material fall to her waist. She was bare beneath. No bra. Only her gorgeous, pale breasts with the big nipples, fat tips and the damned rings. My mouth watered to suck on one.

From behind, King kissed the juncture of her neck and shoulder, slid his hands down to her hips and worked the dress off. It pooled at her feet.

"Fuck, princess," King whispered. "You're such a good girl. So fucking dirty."

I palmed my dick through my jeans. The sight of her had pre-cum seeping out. "So dirty," I agreed. "Going to the courthouse and standing before the judge without any panties or bra."

Goose bumps rose on her skin and she shivered. It wasn't the least bit cold in the room and I knew it was that adrenaline again. She wanted this so fucking bad, but didn't know what to do. Good thing she had two men in charge.

"Take off those pretty shoes," I said, "Bend over when you do. I want one last glimpse of that virgin pussy."

She whimpered, but did as I commanded. King moved so he, too, could share in the erotic view. A heart-shaped ass, a pink pussy all glossy and slick. Creamy thighs coated in that sweet, sticky goodness. I licked my lips, remembering her flavor.

Once she stood before us, bare from head to toe, King

reached out his hand and she stepped toward him. "Kneel, princess."

She frowned, but did so immediately, her knees cushioned by the soft carpet.

"Spread your knees wider. Good. Show us what belongs to us. Hands on your thighs, shoulders back." King guided her to how he wanted her.

"So fucking pretty," I commented. Those nipple rings thrust up toward us and glinted in the light just as our wedding rings did.

King took the necklace from his shirt pocket, held it up for her to see. It was a simple silver chain with a small diamond centered in the front.

"You're our wife now. The rings on your fingers prove that. But you're also our submissive. We're in charge of everything in the bedroom, but also out of it when it comes to your safety, your comfort. We won't let anything hurt you. It's our job to protect you."

Sarah looked up at us through her dark lashes. She nodded and King continued.

"This necklace is like a collar, a sign that your submission is ours. While others might see it as a pretty piece of jewelry, we'll know your pussy, your orgasms, your every pleasure belongs to us."

"And wearing it is an outward sign that you agree to this, that you submit to us, you give yourself to us, openly, wholly. Completely."

"Yes!" she cried, ready to stand.

King held out his hand to still her.

Moving behind her, he slid her long hair over her shoulder so it fell over her left breast, then wrapped the necklace about her, the diamond settling at the base of her throat. It was a short chain, not quite a choker, but thin. Dainty. Feminine. No one looking at it would suspect the hidden—and very important—meaning.

Once clasped, she lifted her chin so I could see. "Perfect."

I held out my hand and she took it, stood.

"Are you all right?" I asked. If she had any worries, any concerns, any reason why she might not want to proceed even though she'd practically shouted her consent, I wanted to know now. Because while she was a virgin—not for much longer—we'd push her just the way she wanted.

"Overwhelmed, but in a good way. I mean, not even two days ago I thought you two were vanilla and now we're married. It's happened really fast."

That was true, it had. At the same time... "It's been slow as fuck, princess. It hasn't been two days, it's been ten years."

"If you're not ready, we'll wait," King said. He ran his finger along the curve of the necklace. "If you want vanilla, you'll have vanilla."

She frowned. "Why would you think that now, after all we've done. I mean, I had a plug in my butt for three hours yesterday and now I'm naked while you're both dressed. Again."

King chuckled at her accompanying eye roll and my heart lightened. She lifted her hands, one to cup King's jaw, the other to cup mine. Her skin was warm and soft and I breathed in her scent. Tilting my head, I kissed the inside of her wrist.

"I want both of you. I, too, have been waiting a long time. I just can't believe you're both really mine."

"Believe it," I said, then paused, lowered my tone. "Let's talk about a few things while our dicks are under control. Are you on birth control?"

She flushed a pretty shade of pink, the same color as her nipples. "IUD."

"That means, what, you can't get pregnant for five years?" King asked. We weren't experts on the details of all forms of birth control, which meant we'd always used condoms. Every time. The only woman we wanted marked with our cum was Sarah.

She nodded. "Four more years. I won't get into the details of my uterus, but I don't have periods either."

While I had nothing against fucking our princess while she was on her period—no part of her was off limits where I was concerned—this news only made things easier. "Nothing wrong with a working uterus."

She turned an even darker shade of pink. "I'm not ready for a baby. Maybe someday. We can talk about it and I can always have the IUD removed, but for now—"

"For now, we get you all to ourselves," I said, suddenly possessive. I didn't even want to share her with a baby we made. Not yet. Like she said, someday I wanted a whole houseful of kids.

"Neither of us have ever fucked without a condom. Today, with you, will be the first time. I'm clean," King said.

"Me, too. We've got the test results downstairs if you want to see."

She shook her head, her silky hair sliding over her bare shoulders. "I believe you."

I nodded. "Good. Then we'll take you bare. Nothing will ever be between us."

"Okay," she readily agreed.

"Good, now undress us, princess. Now you can have all of us. You might wear that necklace that says you submit, but our dicks belong to you."

## 10

ARAH

THE WEIGHT of their rings was a hefty reminder that King and Wilder belonged to me as I undid the buttons on Wilder's shirt, then King's as they toed off their boots. I pushed the shirt off his broad shoulders, let it fall to the floor, then switched to King. Back and forth I went until they were in just their jeans.

I'd seen them like this the other night, but things were different now. They were my husbands. I could take all the time I wanted and touch, lick, taste. But I didn't want to wait another second to get in their pants. The orgasms they'd given me in the laundry room at Steele Ranch the day before were the last ones and I was more than ready for more. I was horny, hot and needy. They'd been practically teasing me with all the things they'd done everywhere *but* my pussy. It all but ached to be filled.

I got my hands on their belt buckles just as I had before and this time, they stopped me again. I could see their hard cocks pressing against their jeans. Wilder's curved up and toward his waist; if it got any longer, it would surely pop out the top. And King, god, he was so long he had it going down the inside of his thigh. It was like a pipe. King's hand covered mine.

Glancing up, I frowned. Angry at being stopped. I wanted to see them, to touch them, lick, suck. God, whatever I wanted. I could now that they were my hus— King's grip tightened. "Hey! Why'd you make me stop? I thought—"

"Change of plans, Mrs. Kingston Barlow. If you touch my dick, I'm going to come all over your hand. I want all that cum in your pussy. This first time, no touching."

"Are you serious?" I asked, not quite sure if they were teasing me again.

King tugged down his zipper, reached into his jeans and pulled out his cock.

"Oh my god," I breathed, staring at it. I knew my eyes were bugging out of my head like a cartoon. He was huge! Thick and long, the head was mushroom shaped and wide. A sandy-colored nest of curls was at the base and it protruded obscenely toward me. I estimated eight inches long, maybe more and there was no way I could get my fingers all the way around the whole thing, gripping it just as he was right now. It was a ruddy red, a vein ran up the length of it, pulsing with heated blood. The little slit at the tip had a bead of clear fluid and I watched, transfixed, as it slid down the crown. Hanging below the impressive shaft were his balls, big and heavy, proving his virility. When he said he wanted his cum in my pussy, I now knew how much of it he had.

I clenched my inner walls, wondering how he was going to fit. Was he too long? Could all of him get inside me? And my bottom. He expected *that* to fit there?

He took his hand away, but it stood erect all on its own as he tugged on the belt buckle, pulled the long length of leather through all the belt loops on his jeans with a hiss.

"I'm serious. Who's in charge, princess?" he asked.

"You and Wilder, but—"

"Don't finish that but, princess, or your *butt* will be red and hot before we fuck you."

I bit my lip.

"You've forgotten already who's in control here," he said. Stepping forward, he surprised me by cupping my pussy with his hand. "Whose pussy is this?"

I gasped at the contact. "Yours and King's," I replied quickly, my eyes falling closed. While he wasn't pressing in on my entrance, the one they'd refused to get near, his fingertips were *right there*. Without thinking, I rolled my hips and humped his hand.

"So needy. So greedy," King said, watching.

I was. They were so mean not touching me. Filling me. "I need it," I admitted, without shame.

"We know," King said, pulling his hand away.

He went over to his bed, ripped the blanket and top sheet down the bed so it dropped to the floor. His dick didn't do anything but point toward me as he did so. "On the bed, princess. Head on the pillows. Get comfortable. You're going to be there a while."

I wasn't sure what exactly was going to happen next, but at least I was headed in the right direction. Me, naked on the bed, was a start. I crawled up on the bed and settled on my back in the center, my head on a pillow as instructed.

King came around the side, held out his hand. I reached for it and he curled his fingers and gave my palm a squeeze. Then he took his belt and made a loop, wrapped it around my wrist and pulled snug. I frowned as I watched, then he lifted my hand up to the slatted headboard and somehow wrapped the belt so it stayed. My left arm was angled out toward the far corner of the bed.

King looked down at me, tested the leather about my wrist. "Not too tight?"

"No," I whispered, licking my lips. I tugged at the restraint and knew it was secure. That *I* was secure. I shivered, knowing that he was in control, truly now. I was at his mercy. His cock was just a few feet away from me, almost at eye level. Pre-cum was dripping from it now, as if he couldn't hold it back any longer, that seeing me like this was pushing him to the brink. I understood now, because I was so wet, my inner thighs slick as I shifted on the soft bed.

When I heard the hiss of a belt again, I turned my head, saw Wilder had tugged his own belt from his jeans and was looping it like King had.

"What's your safe word, princess?" he asked. I glanced at him, then at King who was stripping off his pants. I'd seen his cock, but once the jeans dropped to the floor, he was completely naked. Now that I couldn't touch him.

Automatically, I gave Wilder my free hand, knowing he was going to restrain my other arm as well. As he did so, I said, "Red."

"Good girl. I assume you've never been tied up before. Do you need to say it now?" he asked, his gaze raking over every bare, bound inch of me as he undid his jeans and worked them over his hips.

"No." I shifted my hips, squirmed a bit, realized I wasn't going anywhere. I was completely and totally at their mercy. And that was so hot. "You're going to restrain me for my first time? This is how you'll take my virginity?"

Both of them stilled, King gripping the base of his cock, Wilder pausing as he worked his jeans off.

"If you wanted simple, sweet missionary, you'd have popped that cherry on prom night," King said. He tipped up his chin. "Spread those legs, princess. Let's see that pussy. If it's not drenched in your sweet honey from being at our mercy, we'll untie you and fuck you nice and gentle."

Wilder started to pull his jeans back up.

"No!" I cried, trying to reach my hands out to him, but all I did was flail on the bed. Yeah, so not attractive.

His hands stilled, jeans resting low on his lean hips, his cock pointed straight at me. He was just as big as King, but thicker. The crown was different, not as broad, but with that girth, I didn't think it would matter. I squirmed on the bed again, this time for a different reason. My pussy ached to be filled by that massive thing. King's, too. And I didn't want nice and gentle.

King was right. I wanted it like this. I wanted to submit, to know they were going to do what they wanted, where I could do nothing but clear my head of all the cluttered thoughts and just feel. Just fuck.

"No?" Wilder asked. "No, you won't spread your legs for us? No, you don't want to be tied up? No isn't red, princess."

I licked my lips. While we'd played, done stuff, heck, made out or whatever it was called— although having two guys go down on you and do some serious ass play including a big butt plug probably wasn't in the dictionary as *making out*—this was different. They were taking my virginity. There was no going back from that. But I felt the heft of their rings on my finger. There was no going back from wedding vows either. While I was the one tied up, I was the one with the power here. If I said my safe word, they'd untie me. I was safe with them with my emotions, perhaps some I didn't even know about yet, safe with my body, safe with my submission.

"No, please don't stop taking your jeans off," I said, my voice remarkably calm since I was so worked up. Wilder grinned and pushed them back down as I continued. "No, I don't want you to untie me or fuck me nice and gentle."

It was King's turn to grin and he began to slide his fist up and down his length, catching the fluid that seeped from the tip.

"You're right, King." Boldly, I planted my feet on the bed which bent my knees, and I slid them wide, then wider still. "I don't want simple, sweet missionary."

They stood on either side of the bed and Wilder reached out, cupped my knee and pulled it toward him. King did the same and they opened me up. Lewdly, especially in the bright light of day. This wasn't fumbling under the covers in the dark.

Both men were looking at my pussy, seeing the trimmed hair, the neat landing strip. I knew my folds had spread being opened so wide and they could see *everything*. I couldn't hide from them. They wanted it all from me and they were forcing me to give it to them.

"Dripping." Wilder commented, his cock bobbing as if eager to get to me. *In me.*

"But not ready for our cocks," King added.

"What? I'm ready. Beyond ready." My hair was a tangle behind my head, my arms spread wide and taut. My nipples were hard and aimed at the ceiling. Every inch of me was open. I ached for them. "Please."

"Ah, she begs so beautifully," Wilder commented to King as if I weren't there. "But she's thinking too much."

"Exactly, which means she's definitely not ready."

Both shifted their gazes to me. "Who's in charge, princess?" Wilder asked.

"You and King." I heard the pout in my voice and I wanted to stomp my feet, but they had me completely immobile.

"That's right, which means it's sounding an awful lot like you're topping from the bottom."

I sighed. I was. But it was so hard! And so were their cocks and I wanted them in me. Now!

Wilder kept a hold of my knee but crawled onto the bed, laid down and settled between my thighs. His hands went to cup my bottom and he glanced up at me with dark eyes. I watched as he lowered his head, flattened his tongue and licked me.

I startled at the heat from the motion, but I couldn't move, couldn't do anything but take the next lick and the next. My gaze held Wilder's, but finally fell closed, too overwhelmed with what he was doing. My eyes popped open when I felt a finger circle my entrance, then dipped inside.

"Yes!" I cried. Finally!

I heard the squelch of wetness, felt the stretch of just his finger as it worked its way into me. Slowly, in and out, mimicking what I knew their cocks were going to do soon.

When Wilder curled his finger in time with the flicks of his tongue on my clit, I tensed, held my breath, stared up at the ceiling. "Oh my god. What. Was. That?"

King chuckled. "If I had my guess, Wilder found your g-spot."

"Do it again," I said, my breathing ragged. I lifted my head, looked down my bare body at Wilder. His gaze was fixed on mine and the sight of him between my parted legs was just so wicked. "I know I'm not supposed to be bossy, but I need that. Whatever, the swirly thing is. God, I *need* you to do that again."

Wilder lifted his head. "That good, huh?" His lips were glossy, his chin shiny. I knew I was so wet but seeing it was really hot. His finger curled.

"Oh, yes."

He did it again, and again and brought his other hand

around, brushing his thumb through my slick folds, then over my clit.

I yanked on my restraints, the feel of his thumb like an electrical current. King cupped my breasts, tugged on the nipples, flicked the rings.

The thumb disappeared from my clit and I whimpered, but within a second, I discovered where it had gone. To my bottom. Coated in my arousal, my back entrance was slick and so was his big thumb. He pressed and the way his hand was, he hooked himself right inside. Somehow, I couldn't give any resistance to keep him out. I stretched around him, felt the twinge of pain, the strange sensations I'd experienced from their finger and plug play before now. But combining it with his finger—no, fingers... he added a second—in my pussy, it was so much better.

"I'm going to come!"

"Good girl," Wilder said. "You're going to come and when you do, King's going to fuck you."

"That's right, princess. I'm going to stretch you around my big dick and I'm going to take that cherry. Pop it nice and hard. Make you mine. Then I'm going to fuck you, break you in and then fill you up with my cum."

I moaned at the words. Between that and Wilder's fingers, I came. Arching my back, I went taut, screamed. I'd never come like this before, never felt so intense, so hot, so bright. I had no idea what it was going to be like when—

"No!" I cried when Wilder's fingers slipped from me.

The bed dipped, shifted as I still came and I barely processed that Wilder had moved away, King settling between my thighs, this time leaning over me, aligning his cock and sliding in.

My eyes widened as he stretched me. Then stretched me some more.

"Oh my god."

I squirmed, shifted, trying to take him all. Deeper and deeper he went as I continued to come. He really did have a pipe in his pants. It felt like I was being impaled on one.

"Fuck, princess. So tight," King growled, his forehead pressing gently against mine. I felt the hairs of his chest tickling my nipples as he kissed me tenderly. "I've never felt anything so good before. You're coating my dick with all that sweet cream."

So much for tender. He talked as dirty as could be and it made me drip all over him even more.

My inner walls rippled and clenched around him trying to adjust as he held himself still. I'd seen how big he was. It *felt* like he was huge. Hot and thick, now I knew why they called it a claiming.

"Why...why aren't you moving?" I breathed after a minute, shifting my legs, feeling the wiry hairs on his thighs against my calves. He was so warm, hot even. His skin was slick with sweat and the scent of sex and King swirled around us.

King lifted his head, studied me. "I just want to make sure I didn't hurt you. I popped your cherry, princess, with my big dick." His voice was deep, clipped, as if it were costing him to speak. I noticed his muscles quivered, his cock pulsed inside me, even though his hips hadn't moved.

I shook my head just a touch, licked my lips. "You did, but you didn't." I took a deep breath, let it out. Not only was it weird to have him inside me, having him on top of me was different. He wasn't heavy since he was up on his forearms, but his hips were pressed against mine. I felt... pinned. Skewered. "My gyno broke my hymen when she put the IUD in. God, that hurt. So I'm a virgin, but it didn't hurt like my friends told me it would the first time. And you're right. Your dick is really big."

He grinned then. This close, his eyes were a dark, stormy blue and his smile was like heaven.

"Let's try something," he breathed, slowly pulling back, the slide of his cock over my newly sensitized tissues had me gasping. When he pushed back in, I groaned.

I couldn't move my arms, but I wrapped my legs about his waist, crossed my ankles.

"I think she likes it," Wilder said, settling onto the edge of the bed. Watching.

"I do." I closed my eyes when King started moving now. Fucking. In and out, a slick slide that hit all kinds of places I never knew existed. "God, it feels so good." But just looking at King and I knew this wasn't all of him.

"This isn't topping from the bottom, really." I glanced up to the right toward my wrist trapped in a belt. "But you've got me tied up. You want me at your mercy. Don't hold back. I'm not saying red. I'm saying green. *Very* green."

King's eyes flared and then he glanced down my body. "You're right, princess. But I don't want to hurt you."

I shook my head again. "You won't. You're big, god,

you're so big, and I'll be sore, but it doesn't hurt. Not like it could the first time. Please."

King glanced at Wilder, who nodded.

"All right, princess. No holding back."

But instead of fucking me hard, he pulled out all the way. I gasped at the slide, then the emptiness.

His hands went to the backs of my thighs as he sat back, lowered his head and put his mouth on me, his tongue going right for my clit. After having him inside, this was really intense, pushing me back into full arousal.

I was thrashing—as much as I could—and crying out his name before he let up.

"That's better," he said, coming back over me. "Now we fuck."

He lined himself up and plunged into me.

I screamed and came, so full and his pelvis pressed against my so-sensitive clit. But he didn't let me ride through it. His hand slid down my leg to my ankle and he lifted it up to his shoulder, changing the angle. In and out he moved, his hips like a piston. Hard, so hard that our bodies slapped together.

The orgasm had me in a steely grasp, never ending, swamping me with feelings. I wasn't sure if his cock was magical or if being penetrated and fucked just felt this good all the time, but it was too much.

"I can't...too much," I breathed. Sweat slicked my skin and his grip on my ankle was tight.

He didn't stop.

"We're just getting started, princess," he said, his voice a growl.

"Just—"

I couldn't think, couldn't process as he brought my other leg up, both up by his shoulders. He slowed down now, the angle making him go so deep that he bumped the end of me.

A mouth settled on my nipple. Glancing down, I saw Wilder's dark head. "Again," he breathed against my heated skin.

I closed my eyes, the sight of them too much.

"That's right, princess. You'll come again, but not until I say. And you'll come with me, milking my dick and taking all my cum nice and deep."

My head thrashed back and forth when a finger circled my clit. "I'm going to come!" I cried.

"No." The one word from King had me whimpering. "Come and I'll spank your ass."

It was too much, *they* were too much. I was going to come. It was like a pleasure freight train, no stopping it. My back arched, my arms tugged at the restraints. I wanted to touch them, to pull Wilder closer, to push him away. I couldn't control anything.

"Shit, princess, you creamed all over my dick. You want to be spanked."

"No, I need—"

"We know what you need," Wilder breathed, circling faster on my clit.

King plunged deep held still. "Now. Come now."

I did. There was no scream this time, only white-hot feeling. King groaned, his wrists almost painfully tight on my ankles. He held himself still, so deep in me. I could actually feel the heat of his cum as it pulsed into me. Filled me, overflowed around his cock and slipped down to my ass.

I could barely catch my breath as I felt the bed shift, the belt about my wrist loosen. One, then the other, until I was freed. Wilder's hands kneaded my arms, my shoulders. I knew it was him because King hadn't moved, his cock still deep inside me.

He lowered my legs to either side of his hips, all but collapsed on me so his head was on my shoulder, his breathing ragged. I brought my free hand down, stroked his hair. I couldn't help the smile spreading on my face, even as I kept my eyes closed.

So perfect.

Carefully, he pushed off me, settled back on his heels. Wilder helped me up, held me in his arms, my legs still wide around King's hips.

"You're...you're still hard," I commented. King's cock was a ruddy red, coated in a thick layer of our mixed cum.

He grinned. His face was relaxed, his eyes sated. "Princess, this isn't going down anytime soon. It's Wilder's turn, but don't worry, this dick won't be neglected. It'll be back in that perfect pussy soon enough."

I knew those words weren't a boast, they were a promise.

"Hands and knees, princess," Wilder said, his voice deep. Eager. "My turn."

When that big cock slid into me, I knew I wasn't going to be neglected either.

## 11

ING

THREE DAYS. We didn't let her out of my house for that long. She also hadn't worn clothes in that time either. Well, she'd worn some lacy lingerie and racy kink-wear Wilder had gone out to pick up at the adult store. He liked to pick out shit like that. I liked to take shit like that off her. And to enjoy seeing Sarah in it first.

Crotchless panties. Red satin. Bustiers and corsets. Nipple chains and vibrators. It was all money well spent. And Sarah had accepted it all, done everything we'd asked of her beautifully. Oh, her ass had been spanked several times—she was too sassy on occasion and she wasn't too thrilled about a vibrating butt plug with a remote control—but otherwise, she'd submitted. And hadn't once said red.

She'd pretty much had a dick in her while she was awake. Mine was still hard. Three fuck-filled days later.

Wilder had had to return to work this morning, so had Sarah. Cricket and Penny had been helpful and filled in for Sarah at the library—Kady couldn't take off from the school—their wedding gift to us so we could have those few days as a pseudo-honeymoon. But even though Sarah was back at the library full-time didn't mean I couldn't see her. Fortunately, I was my own boss and the small building was quiet when I stopped in. I'd intentionally picked after lunch to see my girl; any school group visit would have happened first thing in the morning and the moms with little kids were back home for nap time.

I'd walked through the doors fifteen minutes ago, stamped my feet on the mat to get the loose snow free. The action had had Sarah looking up from her seat behind the main check-out desk and smiling. She looked fucking hot as a librarian. Her dark hair was pulled back in a simple ponytail, her white blouse crisply ironed and buttoned almost all the way to her neck. I remembered how that blouse had been worn last Saturday night, tied at the bottom to hold it closed to cover that slutty bustier.

Yeah, beneath that prim veneer, my girl was a slut for me. A submissive, eager little slut. And she loved it.

And I loved her.

She'd stood as I came over to her, the original wood counter separating us. The library was one of the original Carnegie buildings. Not much had been updated over the years besides carpeting, electric so the building didn't catch fire and so there was internet for computers, as well as the vintage furnace being modernized. I liked it old. I'd come here as a kid with my mom and it really hadn't changed at all. Of course, at the time I'd never imagined I'd be married to the librarian.

And as a teenager, I'd never imagined I'd crook my finger and lead that same librarian into the back room to pull the bigger sized butt plug Wilder had put in her ass this very morning and then fucking her. *There.*

After locking the door, I'd bent her over her small desk, tossed up her skirt and carefully slid the plug from her. Between the plugs and her first ass fucking the night before, her hole was becoming accustomed to being used. This time, when I'd slid in, she'd known to relax and breathe, to allow the lube I'd tucked into my coat pocket and liberally coated her with to do its job.

"Quiet, princess. You don't want anyone to know you're getting your ass fucked."

She whimpered then and her ass clenched down.

"Fuck," I whispered. She was too tight for me to last and I played with her clit just as she liked to get her off, the clenching and releasing as she came destroyed any ability I could to make it last and I shot her full of my cum. "I can't wait when Wilder and I take you together. I'll be nice and deep in your ass, just like this with Wilder cramming that pussy full."

My hand slapped onto the wooden desk beside her as my balls emptied. The thought of us finally claiming Sarah together destroyed me. It would be the ultimate submission.

She stiffened when the bell over the entry door rang.

Carefully and slowly, I pulled from her, watched as

some of my cum slipped out after. Grabbing the plug, I coated it with more lube and worked it back into her. Patting her butt, I smoothed her skirt back down, then helped her to stand.

"The plug will keep all that cum in. I wouldn't want the town librarian to have all that sliding down her thighs while she's shelving books."

I grinned at her sated and slightly dazed expression. She might have just come, but I knew she wasn't truly sated. One quickie wouldn't do it for my girl. And the dirty words and plug would keep her hot all day. She'd be jumping me as soon as she got home.

"You've got someone out there," I thumbed over my shoulder. "And I've got chores to do. Wilder will be by at closing time to get you."

I leaned down, gave her a kiss. Realized she had yet to say a word since I arrived. "Be ready, princess. Wilder's going to want you as much as me."

I gave her another kiss. "Love you."

She smiled, slid her hand over her hair. "I love you, too."

Yeah, that was all she needed to say.


SARAH


"Hɪ ᴛʜᴇʀᴇ, can I help you find a—" My words dropped as fast as my smile when I saw who had come in the building.

King had left and I'd taken a minute to tidy up in the

tiny private bathroom off the back room. But it hadn't been someone from Barlow looking for a book to read, but Karl, my half-brother. He'd never read a book in his life, at least not one without pictures.

"Sarah, you're looking...flushed."

His beady eyes raked over me. In the bathroom, I'd ensured my hair was neat, my shirt straight, my skirt down. But I couldn't do anything about the color of my cheeks or the well-satisfied look in my eye. Well, that look was gone with him here, but the flush remained.

"What are you doing here? I thought Montana was too cold for you."

I turned on my heel, went behind the circulation desk. We looked alike, our hair the same almost-black, our eyes equally dark. Unfortunately, we looked like siblings. Unfortunately, we also looked like our mother. But that was where the similarities ended between us.

Karl was an asshole. Instead of bringing his lunch to school as a kid, he'd stolen a different lunch every day. He'd been in California for high school when I'd gone off to college—my child support money from Aiden Steele ending—and he'd told me he'd only dated rich girls in his class, mooching off of them for rides and food in trade for sex.

I shivered at the thought.

I'd seen him a number of times over the years, too many really, but rarely in Barlow.

He sauntered over to the desk in his three hundred dollar jeans and expensive puffy coat, played with the pencils beside the scrap paper. I wanted to yank them from his manicured fingers, but I'd learned long ago not to show any frustration with him. To not show any emotion at all because he'd feed off it. Just like with our mother.

"I'm in Montana because it's a quiet time at work," he replied.

I arched a brow. "You had a job?"

He shrugged, although it was barely noticeable beneath his jacket. "Mother wanted me to join her," he replied.

"You mean your latest girlfriend dumped you."

His eyes narrowed in quick anger, but he smiled. Darkly. "She changed the PIN number on her ATM card."

Meaning, he was broke.

"And Mother? Why would she come here? I thought she had a thing for some yacht salesman."

He pushed off the counter, went to the seating area and dropped into one of the worn leather chairs. His feet went up onto the coffee table in the middle, melted snow dripping from his shoes onto the wood. Fortunately, it missed the selection of magazines in the center. Grabbing a small towel I used for dusting that was beneath the counter, I stood, rounded it and went over to him. Tossing the towel onto his chest, I crossed my arms, tapped my toe. Waited.

We had a staring contest for all of thirty seconds. I was *not* cleaning up after him. Finally, he sat up, dropped his feet to the floor and wiped up his mess.

"She had a plan for his son. For you."

At his words, I subtly put my right hand over my left in front of me to hide my rings. I wasn't talking about King and Wilder with Karl.

He glanced around the library's one big room. "He's better for you than this dump."

"So she's what, come here to drag me to California?" I was so frustrated I needed another orgasm—and to be tied down and dominated—to relax and forget. "Where is she, anyway?"

He tossed the towel back at me. I caught it easily as he stood. "Meeting an old friend."

She had friends here? I couldn't imagine who that would be. I was just thankful the people in Barlow still liked me after all her shenanigans she'd walked away from. Divorced men. Empty bank accounts. Catty behavior.

No, she wasn't meeting a friend. She wouldn't have come to the middle-of-nowhere Montana to visit a long-lost friend. She never came here to visit me.

"She's broke." I dropped into one of the chairs at the realization. The press of the butt plug had me squirming, so I stood again.

"It's not like you've got money to give her," he countered, clearly bitter.

"That's right, I don't." I replied, rattled. "It was good seeing you, but I've got work to do." I went into the back room again, closed the door and slid to the floor. The plug bumped deep into my ass again and I shifted, straightening my legs out and leaning slightly to the side.

I smiled, the plug reminding me of King and what we'd just done to me. My bottom was a little sore, the plug big enough to remember that he'd been there. That he loved me. Wilder, too.

Whatever my mother was up to, I'd get through it. With them. I wasn't alone anymore.

---

"IT'S TOO bad we're all taken. Karl sounds like a real catch!" Cricket said.

We stared at her across the table at the bar.

"Not!"

My sisters laughed. I rolled my eyes. Cricket had come into the library just before closing and invited me to join them for a drink. Penny and Kady were content with water, but wanted to get together. I'd texted Wilder and we agreed I'd drive myself to the Barlow ranch and he would meet me there. Then I'd sent a quick text with *Red on the plug* and he'd told me okay about removing it and that he was pleased I'd told him.

Now, sitting with my three sisters, I thought of Wilder. Of King. I loved both of them and the secret, dirty sex life we had. Eyeing Kady, Penny and Cricket, I had to guess theirs were just as dirty.

"He's here for money, then?" Penny asked, taking a sip of her water with lemon.

I shrugged, staring at my white wine. I didn't drink much and since I was driving, I was nursing this glass. "He's always gone along with whatever my mother had planned. She's skilled at making money off people and he's learned it from her."

"And you've somehow avoided this bad character trait," Kady pointed out.

I didn't tell them about the child support because I

had no idea what arrangements Aiden Steele had made with their mothers. Cricket had said she'd been abandoned by hers when she was just a baby and grew up in foster care so I had to assume our father had made none with her. She'd also just finished college, working and taking classes for almost six years, so he hadn't left her a bank account for that either. As for Penny and Kady, they made no mention of any money. It led me to believe that perhaps I was the only daughter he'd known of. While he wouldn't have won Father Of The Year, I liked to think he'd have supported them in some fashion if he'd known of their existence.

"And yet instead of Karl and my mother, I'm the one with all the money now," I responded. "I got exactly what my she wanted. Aiden Steele's ranch."

"And sisters!" Kady said, reaching out and patting my hand. "We should do a slumber party. Make up for all the years we've been apart."

Penny and Cricket stared at her, eyes wide.

"What?" she asked, grabbing a small pretzel from the bowl in the middle of the high-top table.

"You really think our men are going to let us spend a night away from them?" Penny asked.

Kady pursed her lips. "Good point. Based on the way Cord and Riley went after me when we first met, I'm surprised Sarah's even here. Or conscious."

All three swiveled their heads my way.

"I have to work." That was my only response, which was pretty lame since I didn't *need* to work any longer. But Kady worked at the school and so did Cricket at the hospital, because it fulfilled them, no longer because they had to do it to make money. I didn't want to touch the Steele money. I'd leave it in the bank for my children, for their college.

I flushed, remembering King coming to my work earlier and having his way with me. I clenched my bottom, feeling sore and very empty. Kady was right. I wanted my men and I probably should be catatonic with all the orgasms they gave me. I was insatiable. I'd been in a sex drought for so long, now I wanted it all the time. Good thing my men did, too.

"Speaking of..." I said, sliding from my chair, "I'm going to head out. I've got men at home waiting to make me unconscious."

## 12

ING

"KINGSTON BARLOW. Took you long enough to get home."

My hands were on the buttons of my shirt, headed to take a shower when the woman's voice stopped me dead in my tracks. "Shit," I swore, when I saw who was sprawled seductively across my bed.

I turned away.

"You don't have to stop what you were doing on my account," Beatrice Gandry Roberts Something Something all but purred. She'd been through too many husbands and I had no idea what her name was now. It had been a few years since I'd seen her and tossed her out of my house. Then, she'd been naked. This time, she was wearing one of my flannel shirts.

Not only was I pissed that she'd broken into my

house, but that was one of my favorite shirts. I was going to have to burn it now.

I wanted to walk right on out of my house and pretend she wasn't there, but I didn't dare leave her alone. Not here. Fuck, she was on the bed I shared with her fucking daughter.

"Beatrice, what the *fuck* are you doing?"

I looked out the hallway window, hands on hips. The view was all white snow and open fields; the stables and other ranch buildings were all on the other side of the property.

"You could at least look at me," she replied, sounding put out.

"You could at least ring the fucking doorbell," I countered. I wasn't being a gentleman and my mother had taught me to treat a woman better than this, but Beatrice was no lady. She was where she blatantly didn't belong. The weight of my wedding ring proved that.

"You always leave your door unlocked."

I did, but that would stop. I'd rather have a fucking burglar in the house than her.

"Why don't you keep taking off that shirt and let's have some fun."

I spun about, stalked into my bedroom. She was a pretty woman, I'd give her that. But she was almost thirty years older than me and been through more husbands than I could remember.

"Get off my bed and get dressed." Grabbing her clothes from the chair beneath the large window, I tossed them onto the foot of the bed.

"I have an itch and you can definitely scratch it. By the

size of that bulge in your pants, I'd say you can do a fine job."

"You don't want my dick. You want my cash. My land. Just like last time. Didn't I make it clear enough then that I wanted nothing to do with you?"

She sat up, her dark hair sliding over her shoulder. My shirt was big on her—she had the similar petite and curvy physique as her daughter—and it slid down to reveal the top swell of one bare breast. I looked away.

The answer was obviously no.

The only breasts I wanted to see were Sarah's. The only woman I wanted wearing my shirts was Sarah. I only wanted Sarah.

"I'd keep your bed warm. Other places around the house, too. You've got long winters here and a man's got needs."

"I'm married." I lifted my left hand up so she could see the proof.

The seductive smile slipped. "When?"

"Recently." I wasn't telling her more than that.

"Who?"

"It doesn't matter who it is. She's the woman who belongs in my bed. Not you. Now get the fuck out of it and out of my house."

To let her get dressed, I went back in the hall, looked out the window again. I heard her rustling around, but didn't dare turn around. I saw a car come up the long drive, recognized it as Sarah's. My heartrate kicked up and I ran my hand through my hair. "Fuck."

I didn't look back, but went down the steps and to the front door, tossed it open.

Sarah came in, all bundled up, smile on her face. Yeah, this was what I'd dreamed of. Having Sarah Gandry be Sarah Barlow and be excited to see me as she came home from the library, kissing me on the cheek with her cold lips, undoing her coat.

"What's the matter?" she asked, studying me as she hung her jacket on a hook by the door. Since we'd married so quickly, we hadn't had time—or let her out of bed to do so—to pack up her things and move out of her house. I didn't care since *she* was here. A sofa or her summer clothes could wait.

"Um, there's something I have to tell you."

"Sarah, dear. What are you doing here?"

I gritted my teeth as I watched Sarah's eyes widen, then all color drain from her face. She couldn't see her mother because I blocked her view, but she knew who it was instantly.

"Mother."

When she moved to the small bench by the door to remove her boots, she paused, her mouth falling open.

Turning, I got a look at what made my wife blanch. Beatrice was on the stairs, one manicured hand on the railing, still in my shirt...and only my shirt.

I ran my hand through my hair again as I glanced down at Sarah. I didn't give a shit about anything else. She was looking to me, then Beatrice, then back. I noticed her gaze was on my chest, not my face. Looking down, I realized my shirt was mostly undone.

Shit. This looked bad.

Sarah dropped down onto the bench, leaned forward and began to undo the laces of her snow boots. Only a few hours ago, I'd had my hands on the tops of those sexy-as-hell thigh-high tights as I'd fucked her ass.

My dick stirred. Shit, this was not the time, but just thinking about Sarah made me hard. I smelled her shampoo from four feet away.

"I heard you were in town," Sarah said to her mother, but didn't look up from her task.

"Yes, we came in town last night. I was just...catching up with Kingston."

"I didn't realize you two were close." Sarah dropped her boot on the plastic tray that was beneath the bench, used to catch the melting snow.

Beatrice came down the steps casually as if she owned the place. "The last time I was in his bed—"

I held up my hand. "Stop."

"What?" Beatrice asked, putting her hand to her chest, looking as if she were the one being put out. "I only tell the truth. The last time I was here, I *was* in your bed. Just like this time."

I hated that woman.

"What do you want, Mother, besides my husband?" Sarah asked, tugging off her other boot. She didn't seem mad. She didn't seem sad. Hell, she just seemed...calm.

Beatrice stilled, then laughed. Hard. "Oh, sweetie, I'm so proud of you. I told you to go after Kingston Barlow and you did. Good job. Think of the trips you can go on, the decorating you need to do to the house. So drab."

I narrowed my eyes. They'd talked about me? About Sarah...what, seducing me so she could get her hands on my money? If Beatrice couldn't do it herself, then Sarah could do it for her.

Was that why she'd been at Hawk's Landing last weekend all dressed in that sexy-as-fuck outfit? To seduce me out of my property?

Another car pulled up. I went to the door, opened it again. This time it was a sheriff's SUV. Archer Wade climbed out of the driver's side, Wilder was the passenger. Thank fuck.

I stepped out onto the porch, left the door open, even in the cold weather. I didn't dare turn my back for too long on those two.

"What's up?" Wilder asked, frowning.

"You're never going to believe this one." I shook Archer's hand when they made it to the porch. "I'm going to need your help."

Spinning on my heel, I walked back inside, the others following.

"Wilder, Archer, this is Beatrice, Sarah's mother."

I heard Wilder swear under his breath, but Archer kept his calm. He had on his uniform and held his hat in his hands, clearly on the job. "Ma'am."

I turned to Beatrice. "It's time for you to leave."

"But it's a family reunion, my daughter and I need to celebrate her wedding," she responded.

As if we were going to uncork the champagne with her in my flannel shirt.

"Archer, I'm pressing charges. This woman broke into my house and she's refusing to leave."

"What?" she squawked. "The door was unlocked. We're old friends!"

Archer raised a dark brow and I nodded.

"Ma'am, since you're family and all, I'll give you five

minutes to get dressed or I'll have to take you in like that."
Archer crossed his arms over his chest, already bulked up
by his bulletproof vest.

All casualness slipped away and Beatrice's mouth
thinned, her eyes narrowed. "Sarah, tell him off."

"No. I'll get your clothes." She walked to the stairs,
turned her shoulder to pass by her mother. "I assume
they're in King's bedroom."

Wilder hissed and Archer cleared his throat.

We all stood there, uncomfortable as fuck until Sarah
came back, a clump of clothing held against her chest.
She went to her mother, dropped the pile at her feet. "Be
sure to call Karl to bail you out."

She turned on her heel and went back up the steps,
taking them two at a time. I heard a door slam and I knew
I was screwed. At least she didn't get in her car and leave.

As soon as Archer took the woman away, I knew I had
some groveling to do. I didn't know what Sarah thought,
whether she believed I'd fucked her mother, not just
today—which looked pretty damning—but in the past as
well. She was hurt and it was my job to make it right. Our
marriage was being tested and she had every right to flee.
It had only been three days and I was about to discover
how strong our love was.

## 13

ARAH

I LEANED against the door of the bedroom Wilder had claimed—there was no way I was going into King's room until I had the sheets burned—took a deep breath and tried to will the tears away. It didn't work. My feelings bubbling to the surface were too much and I couldn't help but cry. My mother. *My mother!*

Oh. My. God. I looked up at the ceiling, put my fingers over my eyes. Pressed and physically tried to hold the tears in.

I wasn't sure if I should be mortified or angry. Mortified that my mother had tried to seduce King. Angry for well...the exact same thing. She had the gall to come all the way to Montana and hop in King's bed, and his shirt. And she'd said she'd done it before.

I hadn't seen a car parked in the driveway, so Karl must have dropped her off. That meant one thing: It hadn't been spontaneous. They'd planned this.

Had King turned her away or had the seduction just started when I'd arrived? Of course, he had. She hadn't gotten him to marry her and the disgust on his face now was indication enough. King wasn't a cheater. I knew it in my bones. Glancing down at the rings on my finger, I blinked against the tears, knowing they meant something. Not the tears, but the rings. King and Wilder both had pledged themselves to me even knowing my family.

But what did King think of me after what my mother had said? While *she'd* talked about me 'bagging' Kingston Barlow on our last phone call, it had been just that, talk. But she'd spun the truth into something nasty, making our marriage into something fake. Something exactly like every one of my mother's marriages.

Like mother, like daughter. I pushed off the door and went to the window, stared at the snowy field, the steel-colored sky.

I whimpered, realizing King now thought I'd gone after him because of his money, because of his land, doing Mommy's bidding. If she couldn't get him, then I would. And did. I was just like her, bagging a millionaire. And she'd been pleased! For the first time in my entire life, she sounded proud of me. And what was absolutely ridiculous was that she'd done it while standing in *his* house in just *his* shirt. Like we'd been a team who had ambushed him. I'd gotten him over the weekend, but she hadn't known that, so her attack had come today.

God, she didn't care which of us got in his bed as long as one of us did.

I wanted to vomit.

I didn't want her praise or approval, I wanted King's. What was I going to do? King surely hated me. Hated both Gandry women. Now he was stuck with me. I rubbed the rings with my thumb.

I had to try to tell him the truth, to make him believe I wanted him. Not his land. Not the Barlow name. I wanted *King.*

How could I do that? How could I get him to listen after what my mother had just shared downstairs? I had to bare all to him and get him to forgive me, to get him to believe.

It came to me with a clarity that made my heart skip a beat. There was only one way. I just had to hope it would work. I'd bare my soul to him and hope he took it, kept it. Treasured it.

---

WILDER

"WHAT THE FUCK, MAN?" I asked, shutting the front door as Archer's SUV headed toward town with Sarah's mother in the back seat.

Snow began to fall, the storm that had been predicted to bring over a foot overnight had begun. I didn't usually give a shit about the weather, especially in January, but the snow meant Sarah's mother wouldn't be coming back, especially if King didn't plow his drive. It also meant that Sarah herself wasn't going anywhere. While her car was good in the snow, it wasn't *that* good.

King ran his hand over the back of his neck, glanced up the stairs as if he could see Sarah. "I'm going to have to get a new bed."

He walked to the great room, checked the lock on the door that went out to the patio, flipped it. "It's exactly what it looked like, except I didn't touch her."

"Of course, you didn't. You'd need your fucking shots if you did."

He glanced at me, grinned, but it fell quickly away. Then he went down the hall and to the door off the laundry room, checked the lock.

"You saw Sarah. She probably thinks I slept with her years ago, that I might have again today if she hadn't shown up."

"She was remarkably calm for a woman scorned," I commented, following him back to the front door, to the stairs.

We'd made a circle of the first floor; everything was locked up tight. We both glanced up the steps.

"I need to make this right, to dig myself out of this shit."

"She'll believe you."

Out of anyone, Sarah knew how fucked up her mother was. Knew she'd try anything to get what she wanted, even fucking a guy half her age. But this was bad. If it were reversed and I were the guy her mother was after, if Sarah discovered the woman in just my shirt, I'd be worried, too. Even though the idea I'd fuck her was preposterous, I'd still panic.

King gave me a look that said he doubted my words.

"She's our wife," I said, grabbing his shoulder and making him look at me. I pointed up the stairs. Sarah was up there. I wasn't sure if she were mad, sad, happy, angry. But she was here. She was worth the fight. "She loves us. Married us. She didn't run. Now let's go fix this."

King took a deep breath, let it out, but he still looked pissed as hell and headed up the steps. He turned, glanced down at me. "Fine, but be prepared to duck. I deserve anything she throws my way."

---

KING

I STEPPED INTO MY BEDROOM, prepared for an angry wife. Instead, it was empty, the master bathroom as well. Only the lingering, cloying scent of Beatrice's perfume remained.

I turned on my heel, found Wilder standing in the hallway. I shrugged, wondering where she might be. She hadn't slipped out; I'd ensured all the first-floor doors were now locked...and would stay that way. The house had four bedrooms. She was in one of them.

Wilder went down the hall, opened the door to the room he'd been sleeping in. He'd claimed it with things from his house in town, made it his. Sarah would sleep with both of us, taking turns.

*If* she didn't want to divorce me after four days.

He didn't go in, just stood there, staring. I moved to his side, peeked over his shoulder.

"Holy shit," I murmured.

There was Sarah, on her knees, hands on her thighs, head bowed. Naked.

The perfect submissive. Gorgeous. Her skin looked milky white in the wintery light from the window. I could see the soft turn of her full breasts and a hint of her pussy, although it was in shadow.

My heart stuttered, stopped. When she lifted her head and looked at us, her face blotchy from crying, it kicked back in.

I'd made her cry.

"Princess," I groaned, pushing Wilder out of the way and dropping to my knees before her. "Oh, baby."

"I didn't marry you for your money, for your ranch like my mother said. I *didn't*." Her last words were almost a plea, her eyes almost desperate.

I frowned. "What the hell are you talking about?"

She glanced away, looked down at the floor. Out of the corner of my eye, Wilder's legs appeared. All I saw were his jeans and thick socks; I didn't dare look away from Sarah.

"My mother was telling the truth. We'd talked about me marrying you, getting my hands on your ranch. Well, *she* talked and I listened."

"When was this?" I asked.

"Over the weekend. After the night at Hawk's Landing."

"You didn't tell her we were engaged then, that you *were* going to marry me?"

She shook her head, her dark hair sliding over her bare shoulder. "I don't tell my mother *anything*, especially not something like that. She'd think I was doing it for her kind of reasons."

"But you didn't," Wilder said, squatting down, resting his elbows on his thighs.

"No."

"Why did you marry me, princess?" I asked, so fucking hopeful for the answer.

"Because I love you. I love both of you. I've loved you for forever."

The vise around my heart finally loosened. "That's right. And because you know we love you, too. That you belong to us. You're ours in every way."

I reached out, stroked her cheek. She tilted her head into the touch. I saw the way she relaxed, that her worry had diminished. I glanced at the necklace I'd put on her. Thought about what it meant.

"I'm the one who should be sorry, not you," I told her.

She frowned. "Why? You've done nothing wrong."

"Princess, your mother all but said we'd fucked."

She closed her eyes, shook her head. "But you didn't."

"Hell, no." The idea repulsed me. That crazy, money-grubbing woman was the last person I'd sleep with. "How the hell can you believe me?"

"For one, you wouldn't have done...what we did in the library earlier if you were headed to meet my mother."

Wilder looked at me. "What did you do to her in the library?"

Sarah blushed, but I wasn't letting her off the hook. "Tell Wilder what we did."

She closed her eyes for a moment, then looked to Wilder. "He...he fucked me over my desk."

"Where exactly did I fuck you?"

She bit her lip.

"Not your pussy?"

She shook her head.

"Your mouth?"

Another head shake. I waited.

"You fucked my ass."

Wilder groaned.

"I heard Wilder gave you permission to remove the plug. Is my cum still seeping out?" The idea of marking her so thoroughly had pre-cum spurt from my dick.

"Yes," she whispered.

"Good girl," I told her. If she were going to be with two men, she had to be able to share and share thoroughly, not just her body, but her words, too.

"Why else do you believe I wouldn't touch your mother?"

She cocked her head to the side. "For the same reason you believed me. My mother doesn't lie, but she spins the truth to her liking. I *believe* she was in your bed, not only now but in the past."

I nodded once, admitted what I had hoped to never tell her. While the woman was a bitch, she was still Sarah's mother. I had a feeling she loved the idea of a mother, but didn't like the one she had.

"Yes. A while ago when she was between husbands.

She had her sights set on me. I made it clear then that I wasn't interested."

"She's out of money. That's why she's back. Why she's clearly desperate."

"Hey," I said, trying to sound offended. "I'm not that desperate of a catch."

That made her smile, the corner of her full lips tipping up, her eyes brightening.

"There's my princess," I added, my voice soft. I reached out, slid my finger along the necklace, knowing she was mine in all things.

She launched herself at me, her arms flying around my neck, her head resting on my chest. I almost fell backward from the impact. Wrapping my arms about her, I held her as tight as I could yet allow her to breathe. I felt the press of her breasts, the softness of her legs, the heat from her pussy, even through my jeans. My lips went to her temple and I kissed her, breathed in her sweet scent, savored the feel of her in my hold.

"Your mother's gone off with Archer," Wilder said, his hand caressing her back. "He'll make sure she's gone and won't bother us again."

"That's right," I added. "I'm done talking about your mother. What I want to know is why you were waiting for us, kneeling and naked."

She tried to pull back and I loosened my hold so she could do so, but only enough so she could look at us both.

"Because I wanted you to know I give myself to you. Wholly. Completely. I don't want to think about anything but your touch."

Wilder groaned. My dick pulsed against my jeans.

I took her hand and lifted it to my lips. "Your finger with our rings is all we need, princess." I kissed them, felt the metal warm from her skin against my lips.

Her dark eyes flared. I saw love there. Need. I saw everything.

My whole world.

## 14

ARAH

"WE'RE PROBABLY the most vanilla doms ever," King murmured, kissing my knuckles.

I arched a brow, tried not to smile. "You restrained me with your belts when you took my virginity," I countered. "That's far from vanilla."

"Perhaps. We'll do it our way, whatever it is. As long as we do it together," he added.

"You looked beautiful, princess, kneeling and waiting," Wilder added, leaning in so he could kiss me.

I rose up on my knees to get closer to him, my breasts brushing King's arm as I did so.

"You're naked. Does that mean you want us to fuck you?" Wilder asked.

"It isn't obvious?"

His gaze went all dark and stern as he sat back away from me. "Is that sass?" he asked.

My mouth fell open slightly, not sure what to say. He'd gone from earnest to all dommy in the matter of seconds.

"I think we need to spank that sass out of her," King said.

His tone matched Wilder's, but the wink had me relaxing. It was time to play. As they liked to say, *thank fuck.*

"Get over my bed, princess, ass out," Wilder commanded. "Present yourself."

His words raised goose bumps on my arms as I stood, did as he wanted. The blanket was cool at first against my skin, but when I arched my back, stuck my bottom out, I heated right up, knowing they could see all of me.

I heard them move, stand, felt their palms cupping my bottom.

*Spank.*

I gasped, went up on my toes. It wasn't all that hard, the swat, but the heat of it quickly spread. Everywhere. I was wet. I'd been wet since the library. My pussy was dripping with eagerness to be filled with their big cocks. My ass did still have King's cum slipping from it, but I liked it. I liked having that feeling of being well-fucked, the cum to prove it, to know they were mine. Only mine.

*Spank.*

"We're going to spank this ass, then we're going to fuck it. And your pussy."

I wiggled my hips in eagerness.

*Spank.*

"It's time to claim you, princess. Make you ours once and for all," Wilder said. "If King took your ass earlier, it's my turn."

I turned my head, looked over my shoulder at the two of them. So big, so virile. While they'd spanked me, they'd opened their jeans, pulled their cocks out. By the size of them, they couldn't fit in their pants any longer.

"I'm like a toy, being shared back and forth."

They both grinned.

"Yup, full of sass," King commented. A hand, which I assumed was his, slid down and over my pussy, the fingers slipping over my folds, then upward to my ass, still sensitive from his cock earlier. "Full of my cum, too." His hand moved away, then spanked me.

I hissed out a breath and groaned, not just from the stinging pleasure of the spanking, but how he spoke of what we'd done.

"Spanking, then fucking," he said.

"And princess, no more talking," Wilder added. "All we want to hear out of you are our names and screams of pleasure. You have permission to come as often and as loud as you want."

They spanked me then, although it wasn't all that hard and all it did was sting and heat, sting and heat until I was quivering and eager.

Their hands fell away, then one returned, fingers slipping right into my pussy, finding my g-spot. I went from zero to sixty in one finger curl and I came. My fingers gripped the bedding and I tossed my head back, tensing. God, it was so good. Pleasure coursed through my veins. They were so, so skilled. They'd barely touched me and I'd come. They hadn't even played with my clit. In the past, it had been impossible to do so without my fingers there, but now...with them? I just had to let go.

The hand pulled away and all of a sudden, I felt empty. I shivered, the sweat on my skin cooling, although my bottom was well-warmed. As I caught my breath, the bed dipped. Slowly, I opened my eyes, saw King, naked, sitting on the edge, his feet on the floor. His cock was curved, long and thick, toward his washboard abs.

"That was just a warmup, princess. Climb on my dick and take it for a ride."

His pale hair was tussled from earlier; I was recognizing he ran his fingers through it when he was frustrated or mad. But it also made him look unkempt, as if he'd just spent the night fucking. I had a feeling we would be now, and that orgasm was just the start.

Pushing up, I stepped in front of him, put my knee up on the bed on one side of his hip. His hands moved to my waist to help me straddle him, hold me up until I had his cock beneath me, then lowered me down.

"You're so big this way," I breathed as he filled me up.

Our eyes were so close together I watched as they darkened with arousal just before he kissed me. Our tongues met, tangled, matched the motion of his cock in me. I rode him—his hands controlled my motions—until I was so hot and needy.

Breaking the kiss, he fell back onto the bed. Crooking his finger, I followed him down as we continued to kiss. My breasts pressed into his chest, my hips rocking slightly now because I had fabulous friction for my clit.

But it wasn't just King who wanted in me. I heard the

familiar flip top of the lube, felt the cool drizzle of it in the seam of my ass, then Wilder's finger. "King got you all opened up earlier with his dick. Let's make sure you're ready to take both of us at the same time."

I heard Wilder's words, felt his finger slip into me, the first one to the knuckle then more, then two fingers, then three. All the while he stretched me, coated me with more and more lube, King kissed, prodded his hips up and in with the smallest fucking motion ever. His hands cupped my face sweetly, even while they we were doing such dirty things.

"Time for both your men, princess."

I felt King's legs part, then Wilder's hand on my bottom, spreading me open. His cock nudged me there, just as King's had earlier. But this time my pussy was filled, too.

Wilder pressed carefully until my body gave up all resistance and he popped inside. I groaned against King's mouth, arched my back. Wilder moved in and out, slow motions until I was able to take more and more of him. Finally, I felt his hips press against my heated bottom.

"Fuck, princess. So good," Wilder growled. "You have both our dicks. Such a good girl taking your men."

"So filled," I moaned.

I couldn't move, Wilder at my back, King beneath me. Four hands were on me, keeping me exactly where they wanted me. Two dicks to bring me nothing but pleasure.

They began to move then, alternating in and out and it was the most amazing, overwhelming feeling. I'd wanted kink. I'd wanted wild. I'd wanted dirty and naughty.

I got it with these two.

But while it was all of those things, it was also perfect. They were mine and they were proving it to me. They both wanted me, every inch of me and were taking it.

I held nothing back. I couldn't. I was completely bare, completely exposed. I couldn't do anything but succumb to what they would give me.

I came on a breathy moan, guttural and deep, full-body encompassing.

I felt King swell within me, buried deep, hold himself still as he called out my name, came. Filled me.

"So tight," Wilder said, propping himself up on one hand beside us. I felt his entire torso against my back. Every inch of him. "So good. I love you, princess. Mine."

"Ours," King added.

"Mine," I agreed, slumped on King, with nothing left to give. When Wilder came with a roar and filled me up, I knew I was complete. Marked, claimed. Theirs.

I was right where I wanted to be. I might be a Steele heiress. I might make the future Barlow heirs someday, but I was just Sarah. Wilder's and King's wife.

And I was content.

## NOTE FROM VANESSA

Don't worry, there's more Steele Ranch to come!

But guess what? I've got some bonus content for you —some more sexy times for Sarah with Wilder and King. So sign up for my mailing list. There will be special bonus content for each Steele Ranch book, just for my subscribers. Signing up will let you hear about my next release as soon as it is out, too (and you get a free book...wow!)

As always...thanks for loving my books and the wild ride!

## WANT MORE?

The Steele Ranch series continues with Lassoed! Read chapter I now!

# LASSOED - CHAPTER ONE

NATALIE

"This isn't a date."

"The client isn't here any longer, which means it's no longer a drinks meeting. We're two adults at a restaurant. Alone." My boss, Alan Perkins, leaned across the table and gave me a sly grin to accompany those words.

I did everything in my power not to roll my eyes. It wouldn't have gone over well. He'd been asking me out since my first day on the job eighteen months ago, but I'd put him off. Over and over again. Until now.

Not that this *was* a date.

I watched as the rep from the local chain of retail stores I'd wooed since January walked away—home to his wife and three kids—leaving me alone with Alan.

I exhaled slowly, folded my hands in my lap and squeezed them together. I could be doing so many things at this moment instead of this. Laundry. A cross-training class. A root canal. The meeting with the client had been important, but now? Sitting here in the fancy restaurant with Alan? Misery.

"I don't think HR would consider a client meeting a *date*," I countered.

Alan was in his early forties. Attractive in that...old boys' club sort of way. He worked out, had all his hair, didn't have bad breath and dressed nicely. He turned heads wherever he went, but not mine. I wasn't blinded by the polish, the money or even the slick smile. I'd heard through the office grapevine he'd been handsy with one of the office cleaning staff, but had kept it under wraps so his wife wouldn't find out. He didn't want to be cut off from her piles of cash, the country club lifestyle or from his job since his father-in-law was the owner of the company.

Being handsy was a nice way of saying he was a cheater. And a sneaky one at that. Or, he wanted to cheat, or thought about cheating. I had to wonder if the employee had enjoyed his advances or repeatedly shut him down as I had. I had to hope she was a smart woman and had asked to be reassigned.

To me, even mentally straying called for divorce. Who wanted to be with a man who even spent time thinking about being with someone else? Fantasy was something else entirely. I thought of Tom Hardy frequently when I pulled out my vibrator, but that wasn't the same as feeling up the people who worked for you.

"...as I said, it's after hours. No work talk."

I blinked, focused on Alan again. *I'd* been straying this time, glancing over his shoulder and catching a glimpse once again of the two men sitting at the bar. Tom Hardy was now bumped down my fantasy list because tall, dark and handsome times two moved to the top. They were sitting down so I couldn't really confirm they were *actually* tall, but they seemed to be. Dressed casually in jeans and button-down shirts, one had his sleeves rolled up, and I couldn't help but notice his corded forearms and big hands.

I loved looking at a guy's hands, wondered all the things he could do with them. Perhaps cupping my breasts, slipping a finger into my mouth so I could suck on it, make it wet so he could brush it over my back entrance, tease me.

Whoa, that was a big, and very naughty, jump.

I squirmed in the booth seat and stilled when Mr. Big Hands' eyes met mine. Dark, intense and full of heat, as if he'd been able to read my dirty thoughts. My heart skipped a beat and I licked my lips, suddenly dry mouthed. His focus caught the attention of his friend and *he* looked at me, too.

Where the first was broody, the second was casual, at ease with the quick smile he tossed my way. Full lips twisted into a wicked grin, his eyes raking over me, settling briefly on my breasts. My nipples pebbled at the thought of that mouth on them, sucking, licking, even giving a slight tug.

I wasn't a virgin. That first time in college had been long ago. I'd learned a lot since then, especially about myself. I was adventurous, confident in my own sexuality, but I'd never considered two men at once before.

Until now. Until these two.

"What do you say, Nat?"

I startled when I felt a meaty paw on my knee beneath the table.

Startled, I moved it away, but the action only parted my legs, which had Alan sliding his own bent leg in between.

My gaze flicked to his and the blue eyes had darkened and the mild CEO was long gone. Instead there was a man who had interest. Desire. Both of which were completely unreciprocated. And he'd called me Nat. No one called me Nat at work. Ever. I doubted he wanted to be called Al.

"Can I get you both some appetizers to start?" the waitress asked as she approached the table, blocking my retreat.

While his knee was just between mine and not any higher, it was enough to give me the creeps. Trying to get my legs back together was an impossible task; it only made his eyes flare and the waitress think I had ants in my pants.

"Let's get the spinach dip and another round of drinks." Alan lifted up his whiskey on the rocks.

"Oh, no. I don't want anything." I lifted my hand, palm out. "In fact—"

"In fact, bring the spicy wings. I like doing things with my hands." Giving the waitress a broad grin, she nodded, her smile plastered on, then glanced at me. The look she offered screamed *Is this guy for real?* Perhaps she could tell I wasn't interested, and not just in the dip. Or what Alan could do with his hands. As if the idea of him eating wings was remotely attractive.

I sighed again, flicked a gaze at the two at the bar. They were talking to each other—not close as if they were there *together*—but glanced my way once again.

Alan leaned in, which pulled his knee back. Quickly, I shut my legs and slid closer to the edge of the booth.

"We'll talk merchandise," he said, surprising me.

I frowned. "What? You want to talk about the new line?"

Reed and Rose was a small, boutique lingerie company. It had been started by Alan's in-laws in the fifties. They'd begun with one shop downtown but had since grown to include three stores locally. I'd been hired as a sales rep to get the items—high-end bras, panties, negligees and other feminine underthings—into chain stores with the business plan to spread regionally and potentially nationally.

I'd had suggestions for a new direction in design, shifting from the staid, trousseau-style items and into a sexier and more sophisticated line, but had been shut down by Alan. Until now. I reached for my briefcase on the seat beside me.

"You want to see the drawings from the art department?" I'd worked for months with them and the other design teams to come up with this new direction. It was a team effort we were all excited about, but hadn't been able to get traction with the higher-ups to make it happen.

His hand landed on mine, stilling my motion. I lifted

my eyes to his as I pulled mine out from beneath his, saw over his shoulder that Mr. Big Hands' eyes narrowed at the action.

"This isn't the place to pull those kinds of drawings out. Right?"

I glanced about. The restaurant was high-end, but not ritzy. It was on the first floor of a downtown hotel, convenient for our drinks with the client since it was near his office. The renderings were hand drawn and tasteful, but they were of lingerie.

"Tell me about them instead."

I took a sip of my water, considered his earnest expression. He seemed to really want to hear about what I'd been working on, pushing for, all these months.

"Okay, well..." I went into detail about the line, the bras, the matching panties, the colors and fabrics. When I started on the demographics and marketing research, he cut me off.

"Is this something you would wear?"

I flushed hotly. I loved lingerie. It was my weakness and the reason why I'd taken the job at Reed and Rose in the first place. While I had the degrees and work experience for the position, having a career in an industry I loved was a definite perk. I'd always liked to have pretty, sexy things under my work clothes, but they were for my satisfaction—and possibly the pleasure of a man I allowed to see them—but not for discussion.

Alan's attention shifted to my chest and I knew then he'd only listened to my pseudo-presentation so he could segue to me and what was beneath my professional veneer. I'd dealt with sexism before. Sexual harassment like Alan's that never quite crossed the line. While I'd had conversations with HR about him, his words hadn't been enough to do much to shut him down, especially since the company was owned by his wife's family.

I never wore revealing clothes. I was cautious about it, especially in the industry. Especially with Alan as a boss. My dress was fitted—I was tall and lean with only small curves—but not clingy. While it was sleeveless, it was high necked and fell to my knees.

"Any professional woman would find the line appealing," I countered neutrally.

Alan leaned in further, the scent of his cologne and the whiskey from his breath had me pressing back into the cushioned booth.

"Are you wearing the black mesh number you described?"

I pushed out of the booth, stood, grabbed my clutch. We were *so* not talking about my panties. "Excuse me, I need the ladies' room."

I fled across the restaurant without looking back, leaning against the bathroom sink, staring at myself in the mirror.

Did I want this? A gross boss who was going to constantly chip away at my resolve? Not that I would *ever* sleep with him, but a formal complaint to HR wasn't going to do much. He wasn't going to leave the company. No way. It was his word against mine, every time.

I had to either deal, or quit.

The harsh lighting over the mirror had me wondering why Alan was so interested in me. My hair was a light brown. Mousy. It curled and in the humid air went every which way. I tamed it, pulling it back in a clip, but it always looked as if I'd crawled out of bed. My lipstick was long gone, but I wasn't going to primp for Alan. He'd notice and get the wrong idea.

My makeup was mild, not much could help my eyes which were wide set and too large for the rest of my face. My mouth too full. Or so I thought. And my figure. I was a small B-cup; not enough cleavage, not even a handful. Wouldn't Alan be more interested in harassing Mary from accounting with her full Ds?

I smoothed down my dress, took a few deep breaths to fortify myself.

Leaving the bathroom, I stopped. Froze, actually.

There, leaning against the wall, were the two hotties from the bar.

"Are you all right?" Mr. Big Hands asked. He eyed me, but not like a lech, but with concern.

"Oh, um. Sure," I replied, giving him a small smile.

"I'm Sam." He angled his head toward his friend. "He's Ashe."

"Hi," Ashe replied.

I nodded, not sharing my name. Just because they were making my nipples hard and my panties damp, didn't mean I wasn't careful. Although nothing about them was sending up red flags on my creep-meter. Quite the opposite, in fact.

"We couldn't help but notice your date and his roving—"

"He's not my date," I countered quickly, cutting him off. "God, no. He's my boss."

Both frowned, narrowed their eyes. Sam was about

six foot, dark hair, strong brow, clean-shaven square jaw. His white dress-shirt showed off his broad shoulders and well-muscled physique. Ashe was a few inches taller, leaner. A Matthew McConaughey lookalike with lighter brown hair, cut longer with a wave to it. Defined cheekbones and close-cropped beard. The two of them ticked off every one of my 'what made me hot' boxes. It was instant, intense and made my mind wander to dark and slightly naughty places.

While we weren't the only people in the hallway—a few other patrons moved past us to the restrooms and the din from the main seating area was a reminder we weren't far from others—I felt as if we were all alone. Their focus was on me, only me.

"Boss? And he touches you like that?" Ashe asked. "Unless you want it, but based on your reactions, it doesn't seem like you do."

"Him?" I laughed. "No, I don't want him."

*I want you. Both of you with whipped cream and a cherry on top.* Maybe just the whipped cream.

"Then leave," Ashe added.

"I'd love to duck out, but he *is* my boss and I'll have to see him at the office tomorrow. And, my briefcase is back at the table," I added the last, suddenly remembering. Crap.

"Sounds like it's time to buy a new briefcase," Sam said.

I smiled, then laughed. They smiled, too, as if we'd shared a small secret. "Maybe. I'll make my excuses, although I would like him to consider my product line we'd talked about."

When they both watched me with interested expressions, I waved my hand through the air, shrugging off my comments. These two didn't need to hear about my work. "I'm used to it. To him. It's nothing."

"It's not nothing. *You're* not nothing."

My mouth fell open at the vehemence in Ashe's tone, the way Sam shook his head in agreement. "Oh, um, well, that's sweet."

It really was.

"We're not always sweet." Sam's words were like a promise, a dark one, and I shifted on my heels, rubbing my thighs together. I could only imagine how not-sweet he could be. Whispering dirty words in my ear as he held my hips and fucked me from behind? Tangling his fingers in my hair as he held my face still so he could fuck my mouth? Grip my ankles as he held them at his shoulders as he slid in and out of my pussy with his big cock?

Oh yeah, I had no doubt they could be *not-sweet.*

"We can beat him up for you."

Now I did laugh at the thought of the two of them dragging Alan out behind the restaurant's dumpster, although they weren't smiling. I stifled the sound. "You're serious."

Chivalrous and sexy.

Ashe put his hands on his hips, angled his head out toward the main part of the restaurant. "I assume you're used to Mr. Grabby Hands. That this isn't your first rodeo."

I rolled my eyes. "No, not my first rodeo and I'm used to him. HR can't do much and now that the client's left, this is now a dinner to him. A *date*." My fingers made the little quote motion.

"You just let us know, sweetheart, and we can take care of him."

They didn't know me but were willing to beat up my lecherous boss. *Sweet*.

"That's the um, well, nicest thing I've heard in a while."

It was. I'd been on a dateless streak for so long that I'd forgotten what a nice guy was like. A nice guy or *two*. They were open and honest, sincere and prepared to drag Alan and his chicken wings outside and teach him a thing or two. I hadn't had anyone stand up for me in a long time.

And I hadn't been so attracted, so turned on by a man —two men—in...ever. Instant heat, attraction. God, the chemistry was off the charts and we'd barely exchanged names. And I'd have rather them *take care* of me instead of Alan.

"We can rescue you, if you want," Ashe said. I noticed his eyes weren't that dark after all, more of a bottle green.

"Really?"

"Sure. Just give us a sign and we'll get you out of there," he added, tugging on his ear like a third base coach in baseball.

I smiled at the motion and copied it, careful so I didn't yank off my earring. "Do this and you'll save me?"

"That douche canoe can paddle his own fucking boat."

I couldn't help but laugh at Ashe's words. Again. I loved the way he was mad for me, that he wasn't remotely like Alan. "It's his wife's job to take care of that boat, not me."

"Married? God, he's even worse than I thought," Sam grumbled. "Sweetheart, you don't seem like the kind of woman who really needs saving. I bet you can take care of yourself, but why should you have to? Why should you be stuck with that asshole just because he's your boss? It's after hours. Your time. You've got two big guys to help you out."

*Help you out.* Yeah, I could think of several ways they could help me out. Their hands on my body, discovering I was wet for both of them. I had no doubt they could make me forget all about Alan with some incredible orgasms. Crazy thoughts. I'd just met these two and I was thinking about sex with them. But the connection, I couldn't understand it, but I was drawn to them like a magnet.

I looked down at the wood floor, ran my hands over my thighs. When had they gotten so damp? And speaking of damp...my panties might be dainty silk, but they couldn't handle these two. I took a deep breath. God, they even smelled good. Soap or woods or something manly. Or, perhaps, just man.

"Thanks. I'd, um...better get out there." I thumbed over my shoulder. I didn't want to go. I wanted to stand here and bask under their honest perusal, open interest and well, kindness. Oh, and just keep taking in their gorgeousness. I wanted to see what else they had to say, to learn more about them than just their names. I wanted to run my hands over their hard bodies, learn what made their breaths catch, what made the bulges in their jeans even more impressive.

Ashe tugged on his ear again, as if to remind me of the signal. As if I'd forget it, or the way his wavy hair brushed his fingers. I wondered if it was as silky soft as it looked. And then there was the smile, the slight turn of his lips, the playfulness. But seriousness as well. One ear tug and I knew he'd—they'd—be there to help me out.

"Nice to meet you..."

"Natalie," I finished Ashe's sentence, remembering I hadn't shared my name, smiled. "Nice to meet both of you, too."

"Natalie," Sam repeated, as if testing my name on his tongue. I loved the deep timbre of his voice, and wondered if it would sound the same when he called it while filling me with his cock.

I swallowed, then smiled. Hopefully, the hallway was dark enough to hide the way I flushed at just his tone.

I gave them both one last glance, checking out every nuance. Not only were they so darn hot, but they were *nice,* too. Sweet, even, but I didn't dare call them that. And then their scent followed me. Spicy, woodsy. Male. Breathing them in made me hot and dizzy and aroused. It was as if pheromones just poured off them and I sucked them up as if I'd been in a drought. Which I had, a sex drought.

There wasn't any more reason to linger, and Alan would certainly start to wonder if I'd fallen in or something, so I made my way back to the table. I took in the new glass of whiskey and appetizers in front of him.

He was shoveling some dip onto a wedge of pita bread as I sat back down.

"I ordered for you."

I watched him take a big bite, chewed. A bit of spinach clung to his lip. He grabbed his whiskey, washed it down.

"I'm not staying." I hooked my hand into the strap of my briefcase.

"The night's young. So are you."

I crinkled up my nose in disgust. Looking over his shoulder, I saw Ashe and Sam back at the bar. They'd lost their stools when we were in the hallway, but they leaned against the wood surface where I could still see them. Ashe was talking with the bartender as Sam glanced my way. Why was I still sitting with this loser when I could be with them?

"I have an early morning workout class." I stood once again, sliding my briefcase across the booth. His hand settled on my thigh as I faced him.

"Just as I thought. Nice and toned."

Aaaaannnnnnd we were done.

I was perfectly safe in the restaurant. I could whack Alan in the head with my briefcase. While the laptop might not survive, it would be worth the sacrifice to ring his dumb-ass bell. I could scream and it wasn't like I was in a dark alley. A restaurant full of people was safe. I could even just walk away. But I didn't want to do any of that. I wanted Ashe and Sam, so I lifted my right hand to my ear, gave it a little tug.

While I'd just met the men, and in the restroom

hallway of a restaurant nonetheless, I knew they'd come to me. They'd rescue me. They'd take care of me.

I *knew*. How? I had no idea. I just knew they would. And it felt really damn good.

Keep reading Lassoed now!

# ABOUT THE AUTHOR

Vanessa Vale is the *USA Today* Bestselling author of over 40 books, sexy romance novels, including her popular Bridgewater historical romance series and hot contemporary romances featuring unapologetic bad boys who don't just fall in love, they fall hard. When she's not writing, Vanessa savors the insanity of raising two boys, is figuring out how many meals she can make with a pressure cooker, and teaches a pretty mean karate class. While she's not as skilled at social media as her kids, she loves to interact with readers.

www.vanessavaleauthor.com

# ALSO BY VANESSA VALE

**Steele Ranch**

Spurred

Wrangled

Tangled

Hitched

Lassoed

**Bridgewater County Series**

Ride Me Dirty

Claim Me Hard

Take Me Fast

Hold Me Close

Make Me Yours

Kiss Me Crazy

**Mail Order Bride of Slate Springs Series**

A Wanton Woman

A Wild Woman

A Wicked Woman

**Bridgewater Ménage Series**

Their Runaway Bride

Their Kidnapped Bride

Their Wayward Bride

Their Captivated Bride

Their Treasured Bride

Their Christmas Bride

Their Reluctant Bride

Their Stolen Bride

Their Brazen Bride

Their Bridgewater Brides- Books 1-3 Boxed Set

**Outlaw Brides Series**

Flirting With The Law

**MMA Fighter Romance Series**

Fight For Her

**Wildflower Bride Series**

Rose

Hyacinth

Dahlia

Daisy

Lily

**Montana Men Series**

The Lawman

The Cowboy

The Outlaw

**Standalone Reads**

Twice As Delicious

Western Widows

Sweet Justice

<u>Mine To Take</u>

<u>Relentless</u>

<u>Sleepless Night</u>

<u>Man Candy - A Coloring Book</u>